Murder on the Mountain

A Rosemary Mountain Mystery

Book Two

Nicole Gardner

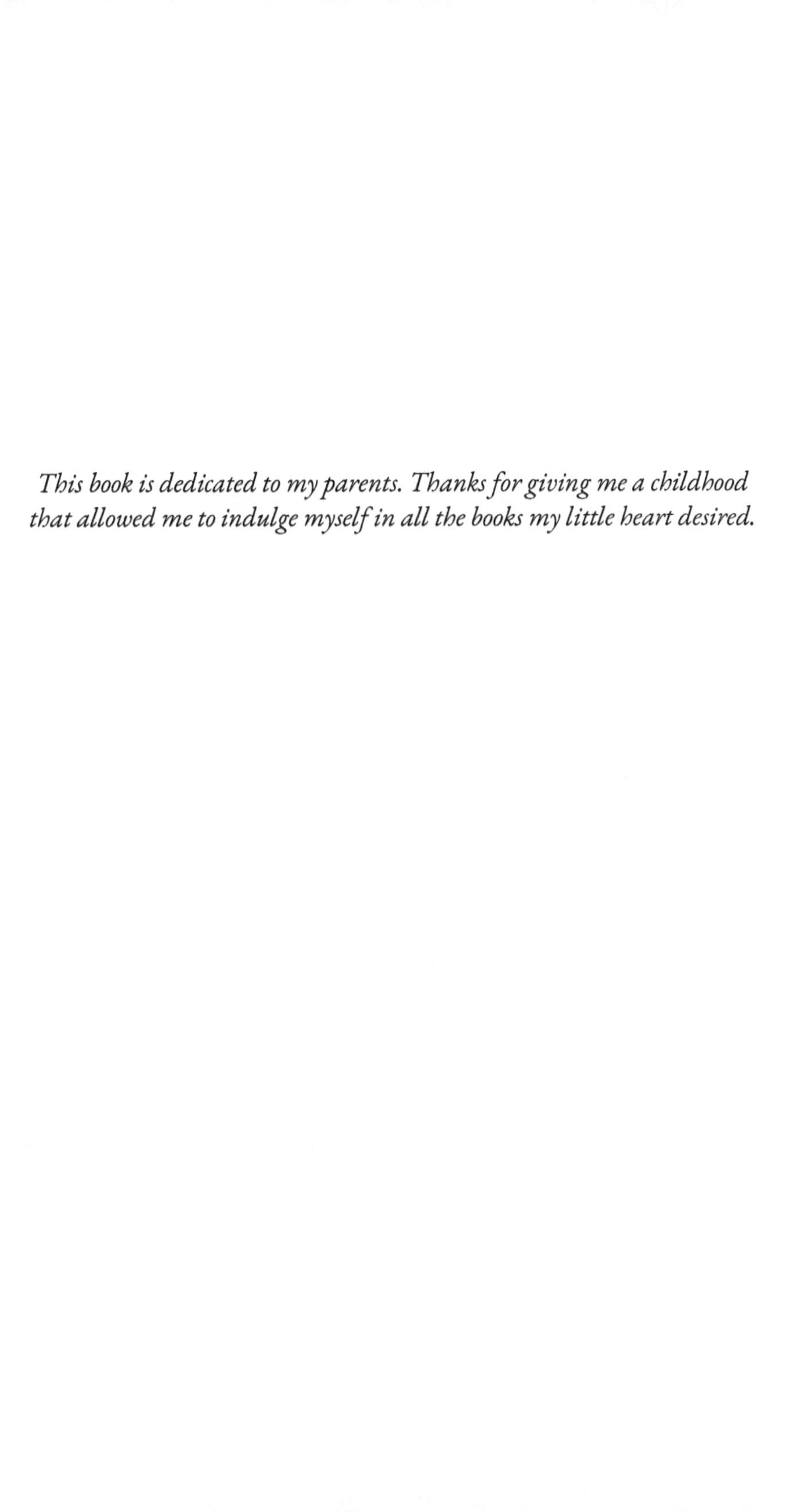

This book is dedicated to my parents. Thanks for giving me a childhood that allowed me to indulge myself in all the books my little heart desired.

CHAPTER ONE

Daphne

Fiona Flanagan was going to kill me. Or I was going to kill her. Either way, it seemed certain that one of us would not survive this hiking trip.

I glared at her back as she effortlessly climbed over yet another fallen tree trunk. Seventy years old—at least that was my guess, as she refused to tell me her age—and she was putting me to shame.

"Have I mentioned you're in remarkable shape for your age?" I called out, panting for breath.

"No need to add that whole 'for your age' thing when you're complimenting me. Seems I'm doing better than you, missy," she cackled.

"You have a point." I leaned against a tree, resting for a moment. Let her get ahead. I didn't care. I could catch up in a bit.

A twig snapped in the forest. I jumped and scanned the trees, wondering what animal had spotted me and decided to make me its dinner. I immediately hit the trail, hoofing it to catch up with Fiona. So much for a moment of rest.

It felt like ages before we reached the clearing Fiona had told me about. In reality, the trail was only about a mile long, but a single mile can feel like ten when you're going straight up the side of a mountain.

Fiona looked at me with sympathy as I collapsed onto the ground without bothering to remove my pack. "Don't worry. You'll have your strength back in no time. Are you still drinking that tea I gave you?"

"I am. And you're right, it is helping."

Fiona was an herbalist, and teas were her choice of medicine. She was trying to get me back to full health after an attempt on my life from which I hadn't fully recovered. But truth be told, even at my best, she still would have kicked my butt on the trail.

"Good, good," she soothed. "You just rest a minute. Get your breath back. I'm going to get started."

She pulled a small digging fork from the large basket she carried on her back and went to work digging up some roots. Suddenly, I no longer needed to rest. I pulled my camera from my pack and went to her, knowing immediately how I wanted to compose the shot.

"I don't know why you're taking pictures of my dirty hands," she protested. Her long, knobby fingers were already covered in dirt, since she hadn't bothered putting on any gardening gloves.

"Because they're beautiful," I answered. It was true. There was something powerful about the image of her hands in the soil, carefully digging out the roots she would use for medicine.

Another shot of her, from a distance this time, then a detail shot of the clasp on her basket. A little thrill went through me. These images were good. Great, even. The long trek up here suddenly felt worth it.

"How's the book coming along?" she asked.

"Slow," I answered after a pause.

She cocked her head, waiting for me to continue.

"I guess I haven't really been working on it that much."

"Now, Daphne Sullivan, you told me it was your lifelong dream to create a coffee-table book of your photography. You're here in one of the prettiest places on God's green earth, and you've got plenty of spare time. What's holding you back?"

I stalled for a moment. "Well, this isn't the prettiest time of year, is it?" I gestured at the trees surrounding us, all stark, empty branches against a gray sky now that winter was coming.

"Uh uh." She wagged her finger at me. "You told me you wanted pictures of all four seasons, and winter just happens to be one of them. And there's beauty plenty in the winter here. What's really going on?" She peered at me with her sharp eyes, the ones that always seemed to cut through me.

I sighed. "I just feel out of sorts, I guess."

"That's to be expected. You've been through an awful lot these past couple of months. But art is a medicine of its own, you know? It would be good for you to focus on it. Might help you get better all the faster."

"Yeah." I looked down, picking at an invisible thread on my pants. "It's just hard to be creative right now, when all I feel is frustration."

She stayed silent, her kind face encouraging me to continue. It was one of her gifts. Fiona loved to talk and could gossip with the best of them. But she was also the best kind of listener.

"I thought we would have gotten somewhere on the investigation by now. Instead, we're exactly where we were. All speculation and no proof at all of who killed my mother. Only now," I added, my frustration growing, "half the people in town are angry at me."

"Oh, surely not half."

I gave her a pointed look.

"Okay, maybe half," she said with a chuckle. "Don and Dave were both beloved members of the community. It's not fair that people blame you for everything that happened, but, well, life's not fair." She shrugged, as if it were that simple. "Try not to let it get to you, honey. It'll blow over. Eventually. And I have to believe we'll find the truth about Eileen when we're meant to. It's why you're here."

I nodded, tears pricking my eyes. The whole reason I came to live in Rosemary Mountain was to find the truth about what had happened to my mother, Eileen. Somehow, I expected those answers to come quickly. Instead, I had gotten myself involved in someone else's revenge, and my whole world had turned upside down. And so far, every answer I had found left me with even more questions.

"I'm also a little stressed about money," I admitted, deliberately changing the subject. "The house in Little Rock still hasn't sold. I guess the market has slowed way down, and it's not exactly what you would call a high-demand property. It needs too much updating. I wasn't expecting to float the payments this long. And with everything that happened, I got behind on my work and lost a few clients." *As in, my biggest clients.*

She nodded solemnly. "Money troubles can wear on you, alright. Do you need money? I don't have much, but—"

I cut her off. "No, no, that's not why I mentioned it." I felt terrible that she even went there. I would never accept money from Fiona. I knew she lived frugally, growing most of her own food and helping as many people as she could, even if they couldn't pay her.

"I'll be fine," I said, willing myself to believe it. "The house will sell, eventually. And I'll find more clients once I prove I'm reliable again. Plus, there's some income trickling in from the estate sales. It's not desperate yet, just stressful."

She came over and gave me a hug.

"Seems to me you've been through more in these past few months than anyone should have to go through in a lifetime." Her face brightened. "At least Emerson is back in town! He should get you feeling better in no time!"

My stomach dropped. "Emerson's back?"

She stared at me. "You didn't know?"

"No." I shook my head in disbelief. "No, I didn't."

I had no idea that Emerson had returned. I had convinced myself that he had moved back to Wisconsin permanently and that I would never have to see him again.

But Emerson Jones was back on Rosemary Mountain.

And that definitely did not make me feel better.

Chapter Two

Daphne

Fiona was obviously curious about why I was completely in the dark about Emerson's return, but I didn't volunteer an explanation. To her credit, she didn't ask, even though it was clear she wanted to.

The truth was that I didn't even know what to say. I was completely and utterly confused as to what had happened between us. We hadn't dated long, and part of that didn't even really count, considering what was going on at the time. Even so, I had thought we were together. I had fallen for him fast. Too fast. But the chemistry between us was unreal, and it seemed, to me at least, that the danger of the situation in which we found ourselves had bonded us more deeply than had we dated for months in a normal scenario.

So yeah, I had thought we were together. Solid. Real. Until he went back home to Wisconsin to reassure his family that he was safe and okay. As soon as his plane touched down, his texts slowed. After a few days, they stopped altogether. His week-long trip turned into two, then three, and by that point, I just assumed he was going to stay there.

But he was back.

And I felt humiliated.

I pushed aside my feelings and busied myself shooting more photographs. Maybe Fiona was right. Maybe I should think of work as my therapy and bury myself in it completely.

I shot some detail shots of the roots she had dug up, then set up another shot of her at work. *Appalachian herbalist in her element.* Her long white hair hung in a braid over one shoulder, and her blue eyes, still as sharp as ever, twinkled as she looked up and caught me snapping the picture. Yes, I could lose myself in this work.

Fiona bent over her own work again, going after another root. A glint of something in the background distracted me as I lifted my camera to shoot another image. I put my camera down and went after the object, intending to move it out of the way, assuming someone had left behind an old soda can or something. I could easily edit the glare out in post-processing, of course, but I preferred my images to be as close to perfect as possible when I shot them.

The item wasn't an old soda can at all. It was a compass, likely dropped by someone out hiking. I picked it up out of curiosity and turned it over in my hands. It was a pretty antique with an inscription on the back that read: *So we can travel the world together. Love, Julie.*

I opened the compass and was immediately hit with a vision of a couple arguing. She was frustrated and trying to get him to listen to her. He was shaking his head, telling her he just needed more time. He walked out, slamming the door.

Reality returned, and I sank down onto the damp forest floor, weakened from the experience. Fiona hurried over to me.

"What's wrong?" She lifted my chin and looked me in the eye, worry written on her face.

"I found this, and then I had another vision." The words felt strange. I still didn't feel quite comfortable with this vision thing, especially considering that this one didn't even have anything to do with my mother. Since the visions had started—or *restarted*, really, since I'd had them frequently in childhood—they had all been related to her and the mystery of her death, and they were few and far between. I'd assumed it would remain that way. Now I was having this random one about total strangers? Uncomfortable, indeed.

Fiona took the compass in her hand and frowned. "What kind of vision? About Eileen?"

"No, not this time. That's what's so weird. I don't even know the people. It was a couple. They were arguing about something."

"Hmm." Fiona frowned again. "Well, I guess we'll find out what it means when we're meant to."

I just shrugged and sighed, starting to feel like myself again—my frustrated self. "Yep. Just add it to the list of things we don't understand. Another vision we can't explain, another mystery we can't solve, another..." My voice cracked, and I despised myself for it. I didn't want to feel like this. I didn't want to feel angry and weak, helpless and frustrated.

Fiona peered at me again. "Honey, I think you need to rest." She gently led me back to the clearing and pulled a bag from her pack. "Why don't we have a little bite to eat and then head back down?"

"But you're not finished," I protested. "You said you need to get your foraging done before winter."

"I may not be finished, but you are," she said firmly. "Now sit down and let's have us a nice picnic dinner before we head back home."

I nodded and smiled, despite myself. There was no arguing with Fiona, so I wouldn't even try. Besides, she was right. I did need to rest, even if I resented it.

WE FEASTED on sandwiches and chips—my contribution to the picnic —and chocolate chip cookies that Fiona had baked from scratch. She had also brought a thermos of hot apple cider, and now that we had cooled off from our hike, I greatly enjoyed the warmth. The temperature was already dropping, with the days being so short. Winter was coming. I felt a thrill at the thought. It would be my first winter on the mountain, and truth be told, I couldn't wait to experience it. Emerson had told me it was his favorite time of year here...but I pushed that thought away quickly. Thinking of him would only bring back my bad mood.

Fiona decided to harvest a few more roots after our lunch, having reassured herself that I was okay. I was glad. I didn't want to ruin her day just because I was an emotional wreck.

As time passed, I became aware of an unexpected issue. I had enjoyed quite a bit of apple cider, on top of the water I had guzzled on the way up the mountain. But there weren't exactly any visitor centers up here.

"Um, Fiona," I said hesitantly.

"Yes, dear?"

"Are you about ready to head back?"

"Oh, just about. This burdock is a bit stubborn, and I didn't bring my full-size digging fork. It may take a bit to finish digging him out. Why?"

"Oh, nothing," I said, feeling oddly embarrassed.

She looked over at me, then died laughing.

"Why, Daphne Sullivan, have you never peed in the woods before?"

"Nope." I shook my head, failing to find the humor in the situation.

She laughed even harder. "Just go off into those trees back there. Squat down. Make sure you pick a spot where it'll go downhill and your feet won't get wet. Look for dirt or pine needles. Rocks or leaves will just splash it right back up on you." She wiped tears of laughter from her eyes. "My, but you are a city girl, aren't you?"

Yes, I was a city girl. But was that who I wanted to be? Not at all. Since moving here, I had dreamed of developing the kind of connection to the mountain that Fiona had. She was completely comfortable in the woods. Knew the names of every tree and native plant. Never seemed to be afraid of running into snakes or bears or anything else. I was fairly certain that if she *did* run into a bear, she would just kindly tell it to move along, and it would listen to her.

That kind of comfort was a long way off for me, but surely I could at least learn this one thing.

It wasn't as if my bladder was going to give me a choice anyway.

Still feeling embarrassed by the whole thing, I searched for a spot that would work. I wanted a tree or a boulder or something to hide behind, with dirt or pine needles on the ground like Fiona suggested. But I also wanted to stay as close to her as possible. Preferably within eyesight. Unlike her, I was absolutely terrified of running into a bear.

Emerson had assured me that bear encounters were rare here, but he had also told me he was on "Team Daphne" before disappearing from my life as quickly as he entered it. So why on earth would I trust anything he said?

Working my way around the perimeter of the clearing, I spotted exactly what I was looking for. Up ahead were some large boulders. Perfect cover to hide behind, but still close enough to make a run back to Fiona if I heard something in the woods.

I quickly made my way to the boulders and ducked around on the other side of them.

My relief changed to horror.

This could not be happening.

Not again.

CHAPTER THREE

Daphne

I raced back to Fiona.

"Well, what in the world?" She placed her hands on her hips and watched me running toward her from the woods. "What's the matter, honey?"

"Fiona." I put my hands on my knees and gasped for breath. "Back there, in the woods. A body. Again."

She stared at me as if not comprehending what I was saying.

"Fiona, it's a dead body," I repeated. "Again."

She appeared dumbfounded. "Daphne, are you telling me there is a dead *human* body in the woods over there?"

"Yes! At least I think he's dead. I didn't check."

She immediately rose and grabbed her bag. "Well, hurry up then, show me where."

I retraced my steps back to the boulders and showed her the man lying behind them. She quickly dropped to her knees and checked his pulse. I wanted to throw up. It was awful enough finding someone dead, but this was eerily similar to the beginning of everything horrible that had happened last month. My whole body was in panic mode.

"Daphne, I do believe we're going to have to stop eating meals together. Seems to be a dangerous thing for the men around here." She chuckled at her own joke until she looked up and saw me. She sobered and led me away from the man.

"Now, now. Deep breaths."

I nodded, grateful for her. "I'm sorry," I choked out. "I don't know why I can't just get it together."

"Don't you apologize for that," she said, patting me on the shoulder as she led me back to the clearing. "I'd say panic is a pretty natural reaction after surviving what you did. But everything's going to be okay."

I nodded, blinking back the tears that were threatening to spill. "Who was he?"

"I don't recognize him," she answered. "He's not a local. Probably someone here doing some hiking. He had a head wound. Might have been climbing those boulders, slipped, and hit his head wrong. Just bad luck. It happens, you know."

"I don't think so."

"Why not?"

"Because he was the man in the vision."

Fiona stared at me, dumbfounded again. "The vision of the couple fighting? Really?"

"Yes." I nodded emphatically. I hadn't seen much, but his face had been clear as day.

"Oh my. Well, that does complicate things, doesn't it?" She shook her head and sighed. "Well, you know what we have to do now. Best get it done. We've got to get down this mountain. And this time, we'll do the right thing and call the sheriff before we call anyone else."

"Fiona," I grabbed her arm, "Greg—Sheriff Morrison, I mean—doesn't know about my visions. And I really don't want him to." *For so many reasons.*

She nodded gravely. "I understand. I've got some fears about you telling people, too. Maybe it won't come to that. Maybe we just let him know about the man over there and not say anything about the other. After all, it's not like you saw him getting killed."

"Right," I said slowly. On one hand, I really didn't want Greg to know. He had already expressed concerns, to say the least, about my mental health. We had finally come to a place of mutual respect, and I didn't want to ruin that by giving him any more reason to doubt me. I also didn't want rumors to start. I was having a hard enough time trying to find my place in Rosemary Mountain, since half the town blamed me for the death of one of their most popular residents.

But on the other hand, it seemed certain that the vision was related to the man's death. Thus far, that had been my experience with what Fiona called "the second sight." Everything I had seen involved death somehow.

The girlfriend in the vision very well might have killed the man. Was I withholding evidence by not telling Greg about it? It felt like a blurry line and I was conflicted.

Then, a thought occurred to me. "Okay. Let's not tell him about the vision. But we can give him the compass and tell him I found it shortly before coming across the body. It had an inscription from a girl named Julie on it. That should clue him into her existence and give him a place to start investigating." I breathed a sigh of relief. I could clear my conscience without getting into anything too personal with Greg.

"Great idea," Fiona agreed. "Now let's get going. Sun's going to be setting soon."

We headed down the mountain, this time carrying more heaviness than just the packs on our backs.

The trip down the mountain felt much shorter than the trek up it, thankfully. The downhill slope forced us to hurry in order to stay upright, and we were spurred on by the adrenaline of what we had just experienced and what we knew was to come.

I periodically checked my cell for reception and was grateful to find it shortly before we reached the trailhead. I called Greg's personal cell phone and explained the situation to him. He was polite and professional, but I could hear the weariness in his voice. The last thing he needed was another death in this town, even if it turned out to be an accident. I felt a pang of empathy for him. He was a good man, and he was as tired as I was.

We made it to the trailhead and tossed our packs into the back of Fiona's truck. The sun was fully behind the trees, and the woods were beginning to grow dark. I felt the familiar uneasiness I always felt here, knowing that soon the woods would be pitch black and the sounds of rustling leaves would be amplified. Greg would expect us to take him back to the body. Even surrounded by law enforcement, I didn't want to be in those woods when they turned dark.

I jumped at the sound of an owl's hoot, then shivered involuntarily.

"Well, that's a bad omen," Fiona said flatly. "Or a good one. Depending on what you believe."

"What do you mean?" I asked.

She pointed at the owl sitting in the branches of the first tree on the trailhead. "The owl there. It's a Great Horned Owl."

"It's beautiful," I said, staring at the owl. It truly was majestic. I couldn't believe we were so close to such incredible beauty. "But why is it a bad omen?"

"Some say it's a symbol of impending doom or death."

"Oh, great." This day just kept getting better and better.

"Of course, some say it's a symbol of good medicine. So maybe I just picked some good roots today. Others say it's a symbol of intuition and foreknowledge. Maybe that's about you. Or maybe it just means there's an owl out hunting tonight." Fiona winked and squeezed my hand, lightening the mood.

At least momentarily.

Vehicles started showing up. First Greg, then some of his deputies. Then Rosemary Mountain police and the hearse from the funeral home. It felt like the worst kind of déjà vu. The trailhead was soon swarming with people, and official vehicles lined both sides of the road. Just like before, it seemed that every emergency responder from the county had shown up.

To make matters worse, I saw a familiar black truck pull over. The one person I never wanted to see again emerged.

I was going to have to face Emerson Jones.

CHAPTER FOUR

Emerson

I FELT THE CORNER OF MY MOUTH GO UP IN A HALF SMILE AS I turned onto Lonely Oak Road. Almost home. I had barely dropped off my bags before reporting to work for a twenty-four-hour shift—the most boring shift in history. Not a single call had come in, giving me way too much time with my thoughts.

At least we had a gym on base. My body ached from the grueling workout I had put it through. Self-punishment, I knew.

Rosemary Mountain had been my sanctuary, my refuge, until Daphne Sullivan had moved there and turned everything upside down.

I had broken my own rule and gotten involved.

Then I went home to Wisconsin, came to my senses, and remembered my rules. But following them meant hurting her, and I hated myself for that.

Just like I hated myself for everyone else I had hurt in my thirty-two years on this planet.

. . .

I PUSHED ASIDE the guilt about Daphne and tried to enjoy the drive up the mountain. I knew this road like the back of my hand. Hell, I knew this whole mountain like the back of my hand. It was my love, the only long-term relationship I would have in this life. And love it I did. I could only hope we got some good snow this winter so I could explore it by snowshoe, before the short Tennessee winter ended and spring came again. Spring didn't feel nearly as comfortable to me as winter did. Spring was all newness, freshness, and life. Spring was no place for someone like me.

I settled back into my truck and gave my dog, Thor, a little pat on his back. He licked my hand appreciatively, then stuck his head back out the window, enjoying the drive as much as I was. Thor was a former Military Working Dog I had adopted when he retired. He and I understood each other. And even though he was retired, he had become something of a mascot at the life flight base. They loved him and let him come with me on my shifts, which was as good for him as it was for me. Made him feel like he still had work of his own. We were a good team.

His ears perked up the way they always did at this point in the drive. Just a few more bends and we would finally be home, sleeping in our own beds after nearly a month away.

But when I came around the next corner, I was met with flashing lights and what looked like every emergency vehicle in the county. What the hell? We hadn't gotten a single call while I was at the base. Had to be a bad car accident or something for this kind of turnout.

My heart stopped in my chest. Daphne lived on this road.

I wasn't supposed to be thinking about her anymore.

But I wouldn't think about anything else until I knew she was okay.

I PULLED my truck over and grabbed my emergency bag. I didn't see signs of a car accident, but it could have been a hit and run or who knows what. If there was one thing I had learned, it was that a scene didn't have to look bad in order for something terrible to have happened there. Best to be prepared.

I told Thor to stay and jumped out of my truck, bag in hand, heading for what appeared to be the epicenter. There was a group of people huddled around what I knew to be a trailhead. The two officers on the outside stepped away from the group, and when they did, I saw her.

Daphne.

Her beauty knocked me off my feet every time I saw her—that long red hair, creamy skin, and dazzling green eyes I always got lost in. I fought to keep my heart rate calm as I walked toward her. She either hadn't seen me or she was purposefully ignoring me. I wasn't sure which was worse. She was standing by Fiona, and they were both talking to my buddy, the current county sheriff, Greg.

Greg spoke to me first. "Emerson, hey," he said. "I'm glad you're here. You know that clearing at the top of this trailhead?"

Of course I knew it. "Yep," I replied, keeping my eyes on him, even though I was desperate to look Daphne over and make sure she was okay.

"Is it big enough for the chopper to land? We've apparently got a deceased hiker up there that we need to evacuate."

I nodded slowly, even though my mind was racing. "Yeah, it's big enough. Want me to put in a call to the base?"

"Nah, I'll call them once I get up there and see for sure what we're dealing with. I just wanted to make sure it was a viable possibility for retrieval first."

With that, Greg turned and walked away, leaving me alone with Daphne and Fiona. My eyes met Daphne's, and a wave of pain and regret washed over me. I had forgotten what it was like when she looked into my eyes. It always felt like she was looking into the depths of my soul, and that for some reason, she actually liked what she saw there. It was a feeling I craved.

Only this time, there was reproach in her eyes. And as much as it stung, I knew I deserved it. I was glad for it, even. It meant she knew I wasn't perfect, and that would make it easier for her.

"What happened?" I asked, even though I knew I shouldn't start a conversation. "Are you okay?"

"We're fine," she answered in clipped tones. It stung again. I embraced the sting.

"We were up there gathering roots." Fiona jumped in, grabbing my arm so that I couldn't easily leave. "And Daphne here went into the woods to pee—"

I stole a glance at Daphne, who was blushing furiously. I had to stifle a grin. She was so cute when she was embarrassed. *Not that I should be thinking about that.*

"—and when she did, she found a dead man behind some boulders! Can you believe it?"

"I can believe just about anything when Daphne's involved." The words escaped before I could stop them. Daphne looked up quickly and met my eyes again, that same reproach in them. I looked away this time.

"Well, if you two are okay," I said, easing my way back.

"Oh, could you do me a favor?" Fiona asked, grabbing onto my arm again.

It was impossible to say no to Fiona.

"Sure. What do you need?"

This time, she grabbed Daphne by the arm, too. "Can you drive Daphne home for me? We took my truck, as you can see, and I'm going to be tied up here for a while. Greg hasn't been on this trail, see, so I've got to show him the way up to that body. And Daphne doesn't need to walk all the way home in the dark."

"But, Fiona," Daphne protested. "I need to go back up the trail with you and Greg. I was there too."

"Nonsense. We both know you'll be scared to death on that trail in the darkness, and there's no need for both of us to lead the way. Emerson here can take you home, and you can finally get that rest you need." Fiona smiled sweetly, first at Daphne, then at me.

I was pretty sure we had both just been handled.

Daphne looked furious, but I knew her well enough to know Fiona was right. Daphne wouldn't want to be out here in the dark. I could at least make sure she made it home safely.

"I can drive you home," I said quietly. "It's no problem."

Her eyes met mine again, and this time I could see the hurt. She nodded silently, then walked toward Fiona's truck.

"Probably grabbing her pack," Fiona explained. "Now, I don't know what happened between you two, and it's none of my business. But it's clear as day that there's some sort of misunderstanding going on. Why don't you try to make it right?" She patted my arm in her grandmotherly way.

What she didn't realize was that I had already made things right.

I had made them right by walking away.

Chapter Five

Daphne

I GRABBED MY PACK AND WALKED BACK TO EMERSON, struggling with my feelings. I was grateful for the ride home, but I hated that he was the one giving it to me. I was humiliated, hurt, and didn't want to face him. At the same time, part of me couldn't help but feel a little glad to see him again. That tiny part of me hoped there had been some misunderstanding, that he would tell me his phone had died or something.

Part of me hoped that there was a reason—any reason—for him ghosting me other than me not being enough. That he would give me an explanation, apologize, and we could pick up where we left off.

But he didn't say a word.

It was all the answer I needed.

We stood beside each other in silence for a moment, watching the scene play out in front of us. I couldn't help but remember the last time we had done this. I had sunk into his comfort that time, with his arm around me. This time, there was an invisible wall between us, so real and so thick that it felt impossible to break. I stared ahead, pretending not to notice.

"You're cold," he said quietly. "Here."

He took off his fleece jacket and held it out for me. I just stared at it for a second. It was such a classic Emerson thing to do, the kind of thing that had made me melt when we were dating. But back then, I thought he did it because I was special to him.

Now, I knew I'd been wrong. I wasn't special to him at all.

"I'm fine," I said, even though I wasn't. There was no way I was going to put on his jacket. No way I could handle being enveloped in something that smelled like him—like sandalwood soap and cedar.

It was hard enough just standing this close to him.

"Daphne," he said, his voice still quiet. "You're shaking. You didn't dress for the evening temperature drop. Just take it."

I looked back at him, my eyes as sharp as daggers. "I'm fine. I just want to get home."

"Okay." He withdrew the jacket but didn't put it on.

He seemed hurt.

I didn't care.

I turned and walked to his truck, not bothering to look behind me to see if he was following. He still managed to reach it a step ahead of me.

"My dog's in here," he said, grabbing the handle of the truck before I could. "Let me just tell him to get in the back."

He opened the door, revealing the most beautiful German Shepherd I had ever seen. I knew he had mentioned having animals, but I had never met any of them. This one was a little intimidating, but when he gave it a command, the dog immediately turned and went to the back-seat. Impressive.

Emerson turned back to me and opened the door wider so I could climb in. I noticed he was very deliberate about not touching me as I did, and I couldn't help but miss the feel of his hand on my spine. I thought not hearing from him was the worst feeling in the world, but this was infinitely harder. Being near him but not with him? It was an ache like I had never felt before.

That ache was dangerous because it was stronger than my anger.

Emerson was silent as he put the truck into reverse and started backing out onto the road. I told myself to stay silent too, but the ache was taking over. Now that we were alone together, all I wanted was to connect with him somehow. I warred within myself until finally, I had to speak.

"How was your trip to Wisconsin?" I asked somewhat timidly. It was the best thing I could think of to say under the circumstances.

He hesitated for just a moment before answering. "It was good," he said, his tone measured. "It was great to see everyone."

Silence again.

"Christie had her baby while you were gone," I said, trying again to bridge some sort of connection. Why I kept trying, I don't know. Maybe I'm a glutton for punishment.

"Yeah, Greg told me," he said.

Silence again.

Then, before I could stop myself, I blurted out the question I had promised myself I wouldn't ask. "Why did you stop texting me? I don't understand what happened. Did I say something wrong?"

He gave a deep sigh, but didn't answer right away. We pulled into my driveway, and he put the car in park, staring ahead before finally turning to me.

"No, Daphne, you didn't say anything wrong. You didn't do anything wrong at all."

"So what then? Is this one of those 'it's not you, it's me' sort of things? What happened?"

"We went on a few dates. It was fun. But I'm not looking for a relationship. I apologize if I gave you the impression that I was."

Of all the things he could have said, nothing could have stunned me more. A few dates? Some *fun*?

"I see," I said stiffly. "I guess you're right. It was just a few dates. You never said you wanted more than that."

I climbed out of the truck, but turned back to him while the door was still open.

"I guess what confuses me, though, is that I thought we were at least friends. But I guess I made an assumption there, too."

And with that, I slammed the door and walked up the driveway to my house.

Alone.

. . .

I felt more frustrated than ever, so I decided to call Joe, the retired sheriff who lived on our road and was helping me quietly investigate my mother's death. Or so I thought. He hadn't updated me at all in over two weeks. Maybe I had made some "assumptions" there, too. I called him for an update, but he said we should talk in person.

An hour later, he showed up on my doorstep with pizza. "Bit of excitement down the road," he commented when I opened the door.

"Yeah. Fiona and I were hiking and found a dead man in the woods."

"Good one," he chuckled.

"I'm serious."

His eyes widened. "I'm grateful you waited until I retired to move here. You and Fiona are always getting into trouble."

I rolled my eyes and invited him in. I caught him up to speed on what had happened, including the vision of the girlfriend. Joe was one of the few people who knew about my second sight. In fact, my mother had used hers to help him out on investigations years ago.

I asked him, as the former sheriff, if he thought I needed to tell Greg about the vision.

"Nah, I wouldn't," he said, before taking a giant bite of pizza.

"Is that just because you want to sabotage Greg's investigation?" I was only half-teasing. You could cut the tension between them with a knife.

He let out a deep laugh at that one. "No sabotage involved. If there was a girlfriend, she'll automatically be on his radar anyway. And I don't want you bringing more people into the loop about your abilities until we know for sure what happened to your ma."

"That's what I wanted to talk to you about. Joe, it's been weeks since you said you were going to look into things for me, and you've kept me completely in the dark since. I'm going crazy over here." I paced the floor, my frustration taking over.

"Investigations take time," he said in his annoyingly patient way. He took another bite of pizza like he had all the time in the world, then calmly wiped his mouth with his napkin.

"I get that," I said, still pacing. "But you haven't even told me anything. At least tell me what you've found out. Have you figured out who Mr. Boddy is? What about getting me an interview with Katie?"

"Daphne," he said, leaning forward. "Your mother died over twenty years ago. This case is colder than cold, since it was never officially a case. It's going to take time. I'm working on it. Carefully and quietly, which, if you remember, is to protect you. We don't know anything for sure yet. But if you're right that your mother was murdered by someone with more power than Don Kistler held in this town, then we have to watch our step. I'd never forgive myself if something happened to you. I already failed your ma once."

I stopped pacing and collapsed into the chair across from him with a groan.

"I know. But it's killing me to not *do* anything."

"You're doing exactly what you need to be doing," he said, reaching for a second slice. "Your job is to stay quiet, act normal. Pretend you've accepted that your mother committed suicide. For heaven's sake, don't go investigating or accusing anyone else. Let me do my job. And if I come across a situation where your particular skills will come in handy, then I'll call you in."

I sighed. "You could at least let me talk to Katie. She knows something more. I know it. Just let me talk to her."

He shook his head firmly. "That's a terrible idea, especially right now."

"Why?"

"It just is." He stood up to leave. "Keep the rest of the pizza. I need to watch my waistline." He grinned as he patted his stomach. I just rolled my eyes. Like Fiona, he was in insanely good shape for his age. This mountain life had kept them both trim, sharp, and young at heart.

I said goodbye to him, then snagged a slice of pizza for myself before putting the box in the fridge. I felt better having talked to him. He always had that effect on me. I would vent, he would stay annoyingly calm and patient. Almost like a grandfather, an experience which I never had growing up. I always gave him a hard time, but the truth was that I had grown quite fond of him and our little meetings.

I changed into pajamas and tidied up for the night. Just as I crawled into bed with a good book, my phone rang.

Greg.

My stomach clenched automatically.

"Hello?" I answered.

"Daphne, this is Sheriff Morrison. Can you come to my office first thing in the morning? I need to ask you some questions."

Sheriff Morrison. So we're being formal again.

"Yes. Is nine okay?"

"That will be fine." He disconnected the call, and I stared at my phone in shock.

This all felt way too familiar.

Here we go again.

Chapter Six

Daphne

I was a bundle of nerves the next morning. I couldn't even drink my coffee. It was irrational, I knew. Nobody was poisoning me this time around. Even so, the similarities between what was happening now and what had happened a few weeks ago had my body on high alert.

If I didn't love this mountain so much…

My nerves grew even worse when I reached the county sheriff's office—and detention center. My own "lock up" had only lasted a few hours, but the thought of it made me ill just the same. I trembled as I walked down the hallway to Greg's door.

"Come on in," he called, spotting me through the glass. His tone was friendly. I relaxed, just a little, until I remembered that he had been friendly last time around, too.

Right before telling me he was getting a search warrant for my house.

"Daphne Sullivan, meet Detective Ford," he said, gesturing to the man standing beside him. I remembered him. He had questioned me a few weeks ago. I didn't remember him being called a detective then though.

"We've met." The man gave me a friendly smile.

"I remember you," I said, reaching out to shake his outstretched hand. "You helped investigate Don's murder."

"That's right," Greg said. "And now he's been promoted. He's part of our new dedicated investigative division. Never needed that sort of thing until you moved here." He winked, showing me he was teasing, but I still blushed. "Anyway, he's taking point on this. I'll let him fill you in on what's going on." He stood up, dismissing us both, and throwing me even more off balance than I already was.

"Right this way." Detective Ford grabbed the door and held it for me, then opened the door to a room across the hall. "We can chat here."

If I was nervous before, I was petrified now.

He pulled out my chair, then walked around the table to sit across from me and opened the file he was holding.

I gripped the sides of my chair. "Do I need a lawyer?"

He looked up in surprise. "What? No. I'm just hoping you can answer some questions for me."

I wasn't sure I could trust that. "What kind of questions?"

"Did you recognize the man in the woods?"

"No." That one was easy enough. "Fiona didn't either. We assumed he was a visitor here to hike or something."

"So you've never met him?"

"No, definitely not."

"You're sure?"

I was getting frustrated again. "Yes, I'm sure."

"Does the name Wesley Adams sound familiar to you?"

I thought for a moment, running the names of everyone I had met here in Rosemary Mountain through my head. "No, I can't say that it does."

"Maybe a past client or something?"

I was getting more uncomfortable by the second. "I don't work with any photographers by that name, no. I don't always know the names of the brides and grooms, but I didn't recognize him as being in any of the wedding galleries I've edited. Why? What is all this about?"

"You're originally from Little Rock, Arkansas, right?" He ignored my questions.

"Yes, that's right."

"So was Mr. Adams," he said. "And was your address there 12738 Power Circle?"

"Yes, it was." My heart raced faster.

"We found this in his wallet."

He pulled a plastic bag out of his folder and slid it across the table to me. It had a piece of paper inside that read:

October 17th

2:00 p.m.

12738 Power Cir.

Little Rock

My jaw dropped.

I stared at the piece of paper in confusion until the date clicked. *October seventeenth. Of course.*

"What is it?" Detective Ford had obviously seen the realization dawn on my face.

"It was an estate sale. That was my dad's house, before his death." I quickly scrolled through my phone to find the sale advertisement and showed it to him. "He left the house to me. He had a lot of antiques, to put it mildly. I contracted with an estate sale company to help me with his things."

He nodded. "Okay. Do you have any idea why Mr. Adams would have followed you to your new home?"

"Honestly, I have no idea." I was flabbergasted by the whole thing.

"Had he contacted you in any way?"

"No."

"Any weird phone calls or anything at all that didn't seem right?"

I racked my brain but couldn't think of a single thing. "No, I'm sorry. I really wish I could be of more help." I felt a stab of guilt about keeping the vision of the fight with the girlfriend to myself.

"And where were you yesterday morning, from approximately 8 a.m. to 12 p.m.? Just to rule you out as a suspect, of course."

I breathed a sigh of relief at that one. "I was at the Wilson's residence with Fiona. She was acting as their midwife and they invited me to photograph the experience. I'm putting together a coffee-table book of local images," I explained, seeing the confused expression on his face. "Fiona and her work is a big part of that book. They also wanted photographs to keep of the labor and delivery process. It's a thing now. So win-win for both of us. Anyway, we went over around six that morning. She delivered around eleven, but we stayed to clean up and help. We were there until almost one."

He nodded. "Great, that should be easy to verify then."

"Yeah. Thank goodness." I was grateful to have a solid alibi, but I couldn't believe that once again, I was in the middle of a murder investigation.

Detective Ford's face softened. "Hey. It's okay. We'll figure this out." He paused for a minute, as if debating whether he should speak. "Look, I know it's tough moving to a new town. Rosemary Mountain is tight-knit and not always welcoming to new people. And I know it's been rough on you in particular. But it'll all be okay."

I was grateful for his empathy. "Thanks. You're right, it has been rough. And getting involved in something like this will only make it worse."

"Eh, you're not really involved, are you? You didn't know the guy. I'm sure we'll figure out why he was here. It may not have anything to do with you at all."

"Except for my address in his pocket."

"Except for that," he said, laughing.

Still, I felt better. "Hey, out of curiosity, was he here with anyone? If that compass I found belonged to him, then he may have been traveling with a companion." I really wanted to know if they had picked up on the girlfriend angle yet, if only to relieve my own guilt.

He hesitated. "I shouldn't really be discussing the case with you."

"I get it, no worries. I was just curious. You said his name was Wesley Adams?"

"That's right." His brow furrowed as if he was afraid I was about to change my story.

"I'll do a little digging and see if he really was at the estate sale.

Maybe he bought something there. I'm pretty sure Janet—my mom—was present for it. She might remember him. Maybe that will give us an explanation as to why he came here." I had no idea what kind of records the estate sale company kept, but any information would be helpful at this point.

His face was relieved. "Hey, that would be great. Let me know what you find out."

"Absolutely. I will." I smiled at him. I got the sense that he felt just a bit over his head with this one. He was fairly young and wouldn't have had much experience working homicides here in Rosemary Mountain.

He stood up, cueing me that our conversation was over, and slipped back into his professional mode. "Thanks for coming in, Ms. Sullivan. I'll be in touch if I have any more questions, and I would appreciate you letting me know as soon as you find out about the sale. Here's my card."

"Call me Daphne," I said, smiling warmly at him. Inwardly, I was rooting for him to succeed. I hoped I could be of genuine help—as long as I could keep myself and my vision out of it.

"Daphne." He clasped my hand and shook it, grinning as he did. "You can call me Jackson."

The woman in me couldn't help but notice how attractive he was. Blond hair, boyish grin, all muscle. Other than the muscles, he was the complete opposite of Emerson. Emerson was the definition of tall, dark, and handsome with his wavy brown hair, dark eyes, and lanky build. Jackson was all smiles, all the time, while Emerson only seemed to smile for me.

But I needed to erase Emerson from my mind—and my heart.

Mentally shaking myself, I said goodbye and headed outside to my car.

Only when I was alone did it hit me how odd the situation really was. Who was this Wesley Adams? Why did I have a vision of him?

And why was my address in his wallet?

Chapter Seven

Daphne

The air was even colder, a sure sign that winter was here to stay. As I waited for my car to warm up, I wrapped my scarf higher around my neck. I wasn't looking forward to going back home. I needed a distraction, some comfort. Something to break me out of this rut.

Fiona had told me that a new coffee shop had opened in the town square and everyone was raving about it. My laptop was with me, as always. I didn't have much work to do, but a change of scenery would be nice. Maybe it would even inspire me to take the necessary steps in order to secure more clients and build my business back to a sustainable level.

It sounded perfect. A little break from the everyday. So I drove straight to the coffeehouse to check it out.

Bells rustled as I walked through the door, and I was instantly as enraptured as everyone else in town. The shop was warm and cozy, but somehow also managed to be light and airy at the same time. Sofas and armchairs invited you to cozy up by the fire crackling in the corner. Bookshelves lined the back wall, full of novels available for perusing as you sipped your coffee. Large tables and chairs offered space to spread out and work. And the soft white, yellow, and earth tone colors kept the place feeling spacious and uncluttered. The aroma was also heavenly—all coffee and freshly baked pastries. I knew immediately it would be my new favorite place to work.

There was already a line to order, so I called Mom while I waited. She picked up immediately.

"Mom, hey. I need a favor."

"Hello, Daphne," she said in an amused tone. "I'm fine, thanks, how are you?"

"Sorry, Mom," I said, laughing. "I'm sort of in a hurry. Listen, do you have any records from the estate sale?"

"I have the original inventory list, a record of what they've sold so far, and, of course, the financial information."

"What about the names of shoppers or buyers?"

"Let me check."

I heard her pad across the floor and flip through some papers. "No, nothing like that. Why?"

"I need to know if a Wesley Adams shopped the sale, and if so, if he bought anything."

"Wesley Adams." She repeated the name slowly, and I could tell she was writing it down. "What's all this about?"

Nobody seemed to be paying attention to me, but I lowered my voice anyway.

"Fiona and I found him deceased in the woods," I whispered. "Dad's address was in his pocket. It had the date of the estate sale on it. I'm trying to find out as much info as possible."

That got her attention. "Good grief. Please don't tell me you're wrapped up in yet another murder investigation. Do I need to call Anthony?"

"I don't think I need a lawyer. I have an alibi this time." I stifled a giggle. "I'm just trying to figure out why he came here with my address in his pocket. Find out what you can, okay?"

"Okay. But Daphne, don't do anything stupid, okay? Don't talk to the police without Anthony present, just in case."

"Too late."

"Daphne Sullivan!" She let out an exasperated sigh. "You are giving me gray hairs. I'll look into this, but you have to promise me to stay out of things this time. I'm ten hours away, I can't just come bail you out of jail at the drop of a hat."

"I promise you, I'm trying to stay as far away from this one as possible. I just need to find out why he had my address."

"Fine. I'll call you if I find anything."

"Thanks, Mom."

I hung up just as it was my turn in line. I ordered one of their advertised specials, a white mocha with almond and coconut. It sounded heavenly on this cold day. I finished paying, then turned to find a free table where I could work.

And ran straight into Emerson Jones.

Chapter Eight

Emerson

"Emerson." Daphne's eyes went wide when she saw me.

"Hi, Daphne." I stuck my hands into my pockets and rocked back on my feet.

"Have a nice day," she said, dismissing me with a nod. She marched to a table and slung her laptop bag onto the top of it, then sat down with her back to me. A clear message if I ever saw one.

I groaned, torn between two parts of myself. Well, three, technically. But that third part knew he had to ignore what he wanted.

The other two parts, though? One said I should just get my coffee and leave her alone. She was pissed off, and that was good. Pissed off was better than hurt.

But the other side had heard every word of that conversation she'd just had with her Mom. And it killed me to watch her put herself in danger again.

I stepped out of line and placed myself in the seat across from her. She raised an eyebrow and continued staring at her laptop as if it were the most fascinating thing in the world.

Which, frankly, it might be. I knew that, along with weddings, she also edited boudoir shoots, and I had to admit I was a little curious about that.

Shut up, third side.

"Daphne, we need to talk."

She never lifted her eyes. "We had lots of opportunities to talk. You weren't interested. I think you've said all you need to say."

"Not about us. I heard everything you said to Janet."

That finally got her attention. She raised her eyes, glaring at me. "You were eavesdropping?"

"No, I was behind you in line, and your whisper, well, isn't very quiet."

She scowled, and for some reason, I liked it. Unfortunately, I seemed to like everything this girl did.

"That was none of your business," she said, returning her eyes to the screen.

I leaned over the table and shut her laptop closed, eliciting a look like daggers.

"Maybe you're right. Maybe it is none of my business. But don't forget that I was there when you almost got yourself killed. Both times. In fact, if you remember, I almost died too. Your investigation affected everyone around you." I spoke pointedly, knowing my words would hit a nerve.

Her nostrils flared, and I could see she wanted to tell me off.

But she also knew I was right.

She sighed and leaned her head back, then looked at me reluctantly. "I'm sorry you got hurt. I'm sorry for everything that happened. You know that. I still feel guilty."

"What happened wasn't your fault," I said, more gently this time. I hadn't meant to make her feel guilty. She didn't deserve that. I just wanted her to stay out of things this time. I needed to know she was safe.

She looked at me with those big green eyes, the ones that had drawn me to her the first time I had met her. That time, she had looked scared. Today, she looked weary and hurt. And I was part of that.

"Look, I'll leave you alone," I said. "I didn't mean to make you feel guilty. It just sounded like you were getting yourself involved in another investigation, and I don't want you to get hurt."

"What do you care?" She snorted, but I could see the pain in her eyes.

"I do care about you, Daphne." It came out quietly, before I had a chance to stop it.

Her eyes widened again. Oh no. I had given her the wrong idea.

"I care about you, but—" I stopped short, realizing she wasn't even paying attention to me anymore. Her eyes were wide, yes, but they weren't focused on me. She was staring out the window behind me.

I started to turn around to see what she was looking at, but she grabbed my arm.

"Don't turn around," she hissed. "I don't want her to know we see her."

"Who? What are you talking about?"

Daphne glanced around quickly, then dropped her voice to a true whisper, apparently remembering what I said earlier. "Wesley's girlfriend."

"Wesley? The dead guy?" I was totally confused.

"Yeah. I have to talk to her." Daphne stood up quickly, not even bothering to grab her bag. I couldn't help myself. I grabbed her wrist to stop her.

"Why do you have to talk to his girlfriend?"

She looked back at me, frustrated and impatient. "Let me go, I have to get her before she slips away. She's obviously trying not to be seen."

"So let's call Greg."

"I can't." She bit her lip.

"Why not?"

"Because," she hissed. "The only reason I know it's his girlfriend is because I had a vision of them."

I released her wrist and groaned. She immediately went out the door. I gave myself half a second to wonder how on earth I had gotten myself mixed up in this again, before grabbing her laptop, stuffing it in her bag, and taking off after her.

Chapter Nine

Daphne

I FOLLOWED THE GIRL FROM A DISTANCE, WATCHING AS SHE ducked into a sandwich shop. She was wearing sunglasses, but her waist-length, shiny black hair gave her away. It was definitely the girl from my vision, and I had to talk to her. I had to figure out a way to get to her without scaring her off, though. It was obvious she was trying to blend in and stay unnoticed. Either she was guilty or she was scared. I positioned myself at a table outside the sandwich shop, where I could keep an eye on her through the window and be ready when she came back out.

"You forgot your backpack."

I jumped at the sound of Emerson's voice.

He took the seat across from me and placed my bag on the table.

I bit my lip, cutting off the response that threatened to fly out. I wanted to say something ugly, something that would remind him of how he had given up all right to be involved in my business, but I couldn't bring myself to do it. Everything he had said before was correct. My investigation *had* hurt other people. A man had died because of me.

I still couldn't forgive myself for that. And no matter what my personal feelings toward Emerson were, I knew he was right.

"Look, I have no intention of getting mixed up in this investigation. In fact, I'm trying really hard to stay out of it," I said.

He crossed his arms and raised his eyebrows.

"Really," I said. "But I may be the only one who knows about the girlfriend. Obviously, I don't want to tell Jackson about the vision. I learned from that mistake." I gave a small laugh. "But if I can find out why my address was in Wesley's pocket, and if I can convince the girlfriend to go talk to Jackson, then I'll feel like I can walk away with a clear conscience."

"Who's Jackson?" He frowned.

"Detective Ford. You've probably seen him with Greg. He's one of the deputy sheriffs. He worked the scene at my house."

Emerson frowned again. "He's a detective now?"

"Yeah. He's part of a new investigative division here, and he's taking the lead on this case."

"They didn't need one of those until you moved here." He grinned —a grin I had grown to love so much. It was rare for him to smile, but when he did, it was like the whole world lit up.

I grinned back at him and kicked him playfully. "That's exactly what Greg said."

For a moment, our eyes met, and it felt like we were back to normal. I wanted to stay in that moment forever. But he quickly seemed to realize we had fallen into old ways. He straightened in his chair and cleared his throat, looking away from me. I forced my thoughts away from him and went back to watching the girl.

"She's coming," I whispered. "Just act normal."

"There's nothing normal about this. Or you." His voice was all gravel.

We locked eyes again. I could see the heat in his gaze before he shut it down.

The girl came out of the shop with a sandwich in her hand, put her sunglasses back on, and glanced around.

I stood up. "Hey, can I talk to you for a sec?"

She froze for an instant, then took off running. But Emerson was faster than she was, and he caught up with her in seconds. I ran after them, catching up just after Emerson grabbed her by the arms. I could tell he was trying to be gentle, but she was fighting, screaming for him to let go.

"Hey, it's okay! Nobody is here to hurt you," I said.

She stopped yelling and turned her eyes toward me, frozen, like a rabbit caught in a trap.

"Can we just go sit on the bench over there and talk for a minute?" I asked.

She let out a sob. "I guess I don't have a choice, do I?"

I glanced at Emerson.

"Of course you have a choice," he said, gently releasing her arms. "We're just trying to help, okay?"

His voice was reassuring, and it did the trick. She nodded softly, then walked with us over to the bench. Emerson and I exchanged glances, confirming that we were both on the same page. This girl was terrified. We would need to tread lightly.

"You're Wesley Adam's girlfriend, right?" I asked.

"How do you know that?"

Emerson stepped in smoothly. "Because in a small town like this, we know everyone. Visitors stick out like a sore thumb."

She nodded, accepting that. "Yeah, I was."

Was. Past tense. So she knew.

"I'm Daphne, and this is Emerson," I said.

She hesitated for a moment. "I'm Julie."

"Nice to meet you, Julie. Have the police talked to you yet?" I asked.

"No. But I saw the news this morning. I know Wes was killed."

Emerson and I exchanged glances again.

I turned back to Julie and gave her an encouraging smile. "Why don't you tell us your side of the story?"

"We had a fight," she said, tears forming in her eyes. "Yesterday morning, early. He got mad and left me at the motel. Said he would be back later. But he never came back, and he didn't answer his cell phone. I was there alone all day and all night. I didn't have a car to go look for him. When I saw the news this morning, about how they found a dead hiker in the woods, I knew it had to be him." She let out a small sob.

"I'm so sorry," I said, rubbing her arm. I gave her a minute before pressing her. "Can I ask you some questions?"

She shrugged. It was a defeated shrug, as if she knew she would have to answer them anyway. It was a bit of an odd reaction, considering we were two ordinary citizens questioning her, and she had every right to ignore us.

"This is going to sound really weird, but Wesley had my address in his pocket. My old address, anyway, back in Little Rock. Do you know why?"

She gave me the strangest look. "No. But that is really weird. Did you know him?"

"No, I had never met him before. That's why I'm wondering about it. It was dated October seventeenth, the date of an estate sale at the house."

"Oh, that would explain it," she said. "Wesley went to lots of estate sales. He was a historian. Public history. You know, records, archives, genealogy, that kind of thing. In fact, that's why we're here."

"Really? What do you mean?"

"He bought a journal at one of the estate sales. It was written by a woman who used to live here on the mountain. He was really excited about it, because—" She paused, looking at us warily, as if unsure whether she could trust us.

I was dying for her to tell us more. My mind was racing. A journal written by a woman who used to live here? Could it be? Shortly after moving here, I'd had a vision of Eileen—my mother—writing in a journal. I was sure it held the key to her murder. Fiona and I had turned my cottage upside down looking for it, even ripping up all the carpet to check underneath the floorboards. But we had never found it. Was it possible we were talking about the same journal?

"Please tell us," I begged. "We're here to help you, I promise."

"It seems silly," she said.

"I'm sure we've heard worse." Emerson popped in with a reassuring smile.

That was all she needed. I had to stifle an eye roll. Women always responded to Emerson. *Including me, unfortunately.*

"Well, when he read the journal, he realized this woman had been in a relationship with some famous robber who had made off with a bunch of gold. And reading through it, he felt certain she had buried that man's treasure somewhere on the mountain."

"Buried treasure? Here on Rosemary Mountain?" My eyes widened in disbelief.

"Yeah. That's why we came. We're here to find it."

"What do you mean you came to find the treasure?" My heart was pounding out of my chest.

"Wes thought the journal held the clues to its location," she explained. "It wasn't as simple as a map or anything like that. But he thought the woman was using coded language to describe where she hid the gold. He was sure that if we came here and searched, he could find it. It would make his career as a historian. Can you imagine if he found an actual buried treasure from history?"

"History? How old was the journal?" I was still more concerned with whether it was Eileen's than about any supposed treasure.

"Over a hundred years old. It was written in the early 1900s."

My heart sank. Not Eileen's.

Unless maybe I had misinterpreted the vision? Maybe she hadn't been writing in a journal. What if she had actually been reading one? What if she had discovered the treasure? Could that have been the real motive for why she was killed?

I needed to get my hands on it to know for sure. "Do you have the journal?"

She hesitated, just long enough before answering no that I knew the answer was actually yes. I wasn't ready to push her, though. I caught Emerson's eye and saw that he knew it too.

"You said Wes took the car, and you were stuck at the motel. Did you *walk* all the way here today?"

She nodded. "Yeah. I avoided it as long as I could, but I needed to buy more food. It's only three miles."

"What can we do for you?" Emerson asked. "Obviously, we need to take you in to talk to the detective on the case so you can fill him in on what's going on. But do you need to call someone? Do you need a ride anywhere else?"

Her eyes filled with tears. "Do I really have to go talk to the detective?"

"Well, yeah, you really do," I said. "They need to know all of this. But there's nothing to worry about. I'm sure the motel has security cameras that will verify you were stuck there all day without a car. It's not like you'll be a suspect."

Emerson glanced at me again. He knew as well as I did that the motel didn't have security cameras in the parking lot. That motel made a good portion of its money renting rooms by the hour; they weren't about to ruin that with records of who came and went. He would also realize that the girlfriend who just fought with her boyfriend was certainly going to be on the suspect list. But he backed me up anyway.

"The sheriff is my best friend here," he said in a reassuring tone. "He's a good guy, and he'll make sure you're safe and comfortable while they get all this figured out."

"It's just..." She swallowed hard. "No one is supposed to know we're together. It will ruin his reputation."

I groaned inwardly. *You have got to be kidding me.* Not another affair. What was it with these young girls getting taken in by married men?

"Because he was married?" I asked in the gentlest tone possible.

She looked at me with an odd look. "No, nothing like that."

I breathed a sigh of relief.

"He was a professor at my college," she explained. "And before you say anything, it's not creepy. He's really young for a professor. We're only six years apart, he didn't teach any of my classes, and there was no special treatment or anything like that. We just met in the library and really hit it off. But..."

"That's against the rules," I finished.

"Exactly. We had to keep our relationship a secret so he wouldn't get fired." She swallowed again. "I guess that doesn't really matter now. But I don't want people thinking the wrong thing about him. And my parents are going to kill me for ditching school to go on a road trip with a professor."

"I can't make you any promises," Emerson said. "That's not my place. But I bet if we explain your reservations, they'll do what they can to keep your relationship quiet. Their only goal will be finding who killed Wes."

"And honestly, it looks worse for you if you *don't* go talk to them," I added gently.

"You're right. I was just scared. Plus, we're talking about *gold*. A treasure that could be worth millions. Wes got killed over that. What if I'm next? I thought maybe since we had been so careful not to be seen together, even here, that I could just slip away somewhere safe."

"Why did you not want to be seen together here?" I asked, curious.

"Because when he found the treasure, he knew he would be doing interviews and such," she explained. "We didn't want locals talking about me being with him. That's what our fight was about. I was so sick of being holed up in the motel while he had all the fun."

"I see." So this wasn't just some fun excuse for a romantic getaway. Wes was truly serious about finding this treasure. I had promised myself I wasn't going to get involved. But I had to admit, a treasure hunt sounded like a tempting distraction from the disaster that was my life.

She sighed. "I've made some stupid mistakes, but I guess you're right. Running would make it worse. If you guys can give me a ride, I'll go talk to the sheriff. But can we swing by the motel first so I can grab my things?"

"Absolutely," I agreed.

Because despite my intention to stay out of it all, I would agree to just about anything if it turned out that the journal in question was connected to Eileen.

Chapter Ten

Daphne

"So, who all knows about the treasure?" I asked when we got back to my car.

Emerson shot me a look. "I thought you weren't getting involved," he muttered under his breath.

I gave him a look right back. I wasn't involved. Just curious.

"I'm not totally sure," Julie admitted. "I know we tried to keep it quiet, but there were people he had to talk to about it. He told his research partner back in Little Rock. And here, he asked permission to search on somebody's land. A Bill something or another."

Emerson and I exchanged glances again.

"Bill Brinksley?" I asked.

"Yeah, that sounds right."

Emerson's face was grim. I hadn't met Bill yet, but he had a reputation on the lane. According to Fiona, he was the richest man in town and acted like he owned our little mountain. He was always trying to manipulate the county ordinances to serve his needs, whether or not it benefited anyone else.

Fiona was not a fan, to say the least.

"Did Bill give you permission to search on his land?" I asked, keeping my tone casual.

"Yeah, eventually. After Wes told him what we were doing."

Interesting.

"Is the trail where Wes was found on Bill's land?" I asked Emerson, my voice low.

He shook his head. "That's public land. There are some hiking trails that do cut through private property. Nobody else up there seems to mind hikers, but Bill's property is covered in no trespassing signs. I'm surprised he let them search."

Based on the description I had gotten from Fiona, I couldn't imagine him letting people search for buried treasure on his property out of the kindness of his heart. He must have thought something was in it for himself. If Wes thought it would be a historical boon, maybe Bill was interested in the publicity. Who knew? It was something interesting to file away, for sure.

"So, Bill and his research partner. Anyone else you can think of?" I asked, ignoring Emerson's groan from the passenger seat.

"No. He talked to a librarian here. He went there to research the woman who wrote the journal, looking for more information, you know. But I don't think he mentioned the treasure. He said he would just play it off as genealogy research." She hesitated for a moment. "The only other thing I can think of is that the walls at the motel are pretty thin, you know? We tried to be careful when we heard someone next door, but it's possible someone heard something before we realized just how thin they were."

Well, that didn't narrow it down, unless Jackson could get an accurate record from the motel of who all had been in that room.

I saw Emerson pull out his cell phone to send a text.

"Greg?" I asked, quietly.

He nodded. Good. I was glad to give them a heads-up. Although I would rather have contacted Jackson directly. I didn't want him to think we were going over his head to Greg.

"Here we are," I said, pulling into the motel parking lot. "Which room is yours?"

"B22," she said, motioning toward the end of the building. I drove down there and pulled into the space in front of her room.

"I'll just be a second," she said.

"Hang on, I'm coming with you," Emerson said, hopping out after her.

I had to admit, as much as it hurt to be around him, I was glad to have him here. I knew exactly what he was doing. The man couldn't help himself. It was his nature to play bodyguard. There was no way he would let her go in there alone, on the tiny chance that someone was waiting for her.

When they returned to the car moments later, I knew something was wrong.

Emerson walked to my window instead of getting in. "The place has been ransacked," he said, a grim look on his face.

"Are you serious?" I asked.

"Yep. I called Greg. Detective Ford is en route. We're to wait here and not go back in there."

I climbed out of the car and we walked over to the building, where Julie was now sitting on the sidewalk, her back pressed up against the siding. She looked more terrified than ever, poor thing. I sat down beside her.

"You okay?"

"Just scared," she said. "What if I had been there? What if..."

"You can't think about that," I said. "You weren't here, thank goodness. Whoever did this was probably watching, waiting for you to leave."

She nodded.

"Did they take anything?" I asked. I glanced over at Emerson and caught him shaking his head, with his lips clamped tight. The man really wanted me to stay out of this.

Maybe that's why I kept pushing.

"I didn't look through everything, but Wes's laptop and notebook were gone. They won't get too far with that, though, at least not quickly."

"Why?"

She laughed, then a sad expression crossed her face. "He always wrote all of his notes in some sort of code. He was a nerd. Loved studying old secret codes and ciphers. Everything about the treasure was written that way."

"I'm sorry he's gone," I said quietly. "I know what it's like to lose someone."

She nodded, tears filling her eyes again.

I looked over at Emerson, who had sat down on the other side of her. His own face was etched with pain. He knew what it was like to lose someone, too. He had told me about losing his baby brother, Ken, in Afghanistan. I knew it still hurt. I also knew he didn't like to talk about it.

Seeing the pain on his face wrecked me. All I wanted to do was go to him and comfort him.

It killed me that he wasn't mine to comfort.

"Daphne," Julie said, hesitant.

"Yes?"

"I think you should take this."

She reached into her backpack and pulled out the journal.

Chapter Eleven

Emerson

I watched Daphne's green eyes light up as she reverently took the journal into her hands. I knew she was thinking of her mother and hoping this was going to be the answer.

I hoped she was right, not only because it would give her the answers I knew she longed for, but also because then I could stop worrying about her inserting herself into the investigation.

The girl sure had a knack for getting herself into trouble.

I watched her open the journal and scan the first few pages before a look of regret flitted across her face. She quickly flipped through the rest of it as if checking for something, then took a few snaps of pages with her cell phone.

"Thank you," she said to Julie, handing it back to her with care. "But as much as I want to dive into this, I think you probably need to turn it over to Jackson. I mean, Detective Ford. He's the one working this case."

I felt like rejoicing over the fact that she was actually going to let him handle it. But it annoyed me that she was familiar enough to call him by his first name.

You have no right to her, I reminded myself. She was free to date whomever she wanted. And if it hurt me to watch, well, I deserved it.

But I still didn't like it.

Only a few moments passed before "Jackson" pulled up in his county truck with the big sheriff's logo on the side. He swung out, in uniform, with a grin on his face. I studied him for a moment. Compared to him, I felt like an old man. He was young. Young enough to not be jaded yet. He was everything I wasn't, and I wanted to hate him for it, especially when he walked straight to Daphne with that big grin on his face.

"Long time no see," he joked with her.

"We really have to stop meeting like this," she teased back, standing up to meet him. She quickly gave him the rundown of everything that had happened and all we had learned.

He whistled in appreciation. "You could be a detective, you know that? Might have a place for you in the division if you want to keep helping us out." He flashed that grin again, and I felt my face go dark.

A pink flush rose in Daphne's cheeks at the compliment. I wished I had put it there.

I watched them chat as Daphne introduced him to Julie, and as he reassured the girl that he would do everything he could to find out what had happened to Wes. Daphne seemed relaxed, lighter, with him here. He was probably exactly what she needed.

A hard wave of regret washed over me as I wished it could be me.

Daphne and I hung around during the investigation, but we basically ignored each other. We kept Julie company while "Jackson" and his men did their thing. I couldn't seem to think of him as Detective Ford, or say his name without adding sarcastic mental quotation marks to it.

I needed to get away from Daphne so I could go back to being a decent human being, instead of the jealous, irritable man I'd become.

They finally wrapped up, and Daphne said goodbye to Julie with a hug. "Jackson" was taking Julie back to the station for a formal interview. I noticed him and Daphne exchange meaningful looks. Daphne was clearly warning him that Julie was fragile, and he seemed to reassure Daphne that he would handle things with care.

Just how well did they know each other, anyway?

None of my business, I reminded myself.

"Well, I guess I should drive you back to your truck," Daphne said, interrupting my internal monologue.

"Oh, yeah. I guess we rode together." Which meant we would be alone together on the ride back to it. Alone with Daphne was a situation I needed to keep myself out of. I was tempted to walk the three miles back to the town square.

But since that would be awkward to explain, I kept my mouth shut and climbed into her passenger seat again. Today was actually the first time I had ever been in her car. It was as neat and clean as she was. Even in our short time together, I had noticed she liked her space to be clear and organized at all times.

"Thanks for being there today," she said, her voice soft.

"Sure," I said. I wanted to say "always," but that was a promise I couldn't make.

"I hope she'll be okay."

"It'll be tough, but she'll get through it," I said. "She's young."

"Yeah."

The silence became awkward.

"So, you're out of the case now, right?" I asked.

"What? Oh. Yeah. Of course."

I didn't like the look on her face. I didn't believe her one bit. "Daphne..."

"I'm staying out of things. But, Emerson, what if that was *the* journal from my vision, the one I had about my mother? It makes sense. Why else would I have had a vision of that couple? The journal connects them to Eileen. If he bought it at Dad's estate sale, then it makes sense that it was the same journal I saw Eileen with before she died. Right?"

"Yes, that makes sense," I said slowly. "But if that's what you believe, then why did you give it to Jackson? You could have kept it."

She sighed. "Because I want to be on the up and up this time. No more sneaking around, getting into trouble. And honestly, I thought if it was *the* journal, I would have had some sort of vision just touching it. I didn't. I flipped through it quickly, just in case there were extra notes or something from Eileen. But I didn't see anything that looked out of place. And giving it to Jackson buys me some goodwill, which, in case you haven't noticed, I need right now."

"What do you mean?" She seemed to have plenty of goodwill from "Jackson."

"Oh," she said, glancing in my direction. "I guess you haven't really been around to see. I'm not exactly Rosemary Mountain's most beloved citizen these days."

"Gotcha." I felt a pang of sympathy for her. "Don's supporters rallying against you?"

"His, and Dave's, for that matter. I'd say half the town blames me for the whole thing."

"It wasn't your fault."

She glanced my way again. "And yet it was, as you were so quick to remind me earlier."

"That's not what I meant," I protested. "Look, Don, Dave, and Katie all made their own choices. You aren't responsible for what happened to any of them. None of that is your fault, so stop owning it, okay? That guilt will eat you alive." *Ask me how I know.*

"Then what did you mean earlier?"

"Just that when you knowingly put yourself in danger, it affects the people who love you." *Crap.* "And, you know, the people around you."

"I see."

I'd swear she was fighting back a smile.

"Anyway," I said, clearing my throat. "My truck's over there." I had never been so happy to reach the town square.

She pulled her car into the spot beside mine, then looked at me with those beautiful eyes.

"See you around, Emerson."

"Yeah. See you around," I said.

But for both our sakes, I hoped we didn't see each other again for a real long time.

Chapter Twelve

Daphne

I watched Emerson climb into his truck and drive away. The man was a walking contradiction. First, he ghosted me, acted like he didn't give a damn about me. Then today, he followed me around like a bodyguard. And I saw the look on his face when he mentioned "people who love you." He didn't mean to say it, and looked panicked after he did. But some part of him cared. I could feel it. Could see it.

What I didn't know was why he had decided we couldn't be together.

My mind went back to Katie and the conversation we'd had about him when she'd found out we were dating. "He's not marriage material," she had said. "Have all the fun you want with him, but don't expect more."

What was I missing?

I had two reasons for wanting to talk to her, and I was going to lose it if Joe didn't come through with an interview soon.

But in the meantime, I needed to call Mom.

· · ·

I DIALED Mom's number before backing out of the town square.

"Two calls in one day?" She had an amused tone to her voice. "To what do I owe the pleasure? Or do you need me to come bail you out after all?"

"Very funny, Mom." I rolled my eyes. "Listen, I found out some more info."

"Good, because I haven't found out anything. I called the company that handled the sales, but they said they would have to get back to me. They did tell me, however, that they haven't gotten even halfway through your father's things, by the way. Such a packrat. They're planning another sale next month."

"Tell them to postpone it," I said. "Look, I hate to do this to you, but I may need you to go through Dad's things. Let me explain first, though." I quickly filled her in on everything Julie had said about the journal and the treasure hunt.

"Buried treasure?" Her voice sounded awed. "Daphne, I hate to admit this, but I'm starting to feel a little jealous about how exciting your life is."

"So come back and investigate with me." I laughed. It hit me what an odd thing that was. A few months ago, I couldn't stand being in the same room with her. Things had changed so much since the truth had come out. At least there was a bright side to everything awful that had happened.

"Well, it sounds like I need to do some investigating here first, doesn't it? Why do you want me to look through your dad's things?"

"I want you to see if there are any other journals or letters or anything that was written by the same woman. The name in the front of the journal was Della Porter. I felt like I had to turn it over to the detective in charge of the case, but if we have anything else..."

"I see. You're going after the treasure." Her amused tone returned.

"I didn't say that. But you have to admit, it's an exciting thing to think about." A little thrill rose in me. "Plus, if it has anything to do with Eileen..."

Mom sobered. "I get it. I really do. I'll be happy to go over there and see if I can find anything. But Daphne, please be careful. I don't think I could take it if something else happened to you."

"I know. I promise, I'm not going to get involved in anything dangerous. Emerson has already made me feel plenty of guilt about that today."

"Emerson?" Her tone became more cheerful. "Have you two finally talked?"

I cringed, regretting having said anything. It was downright embarrassing to have been ghosted, especially with Mom knowing just how crazy I was about him. She was crazy about him too. I was pretty sure she would have already planned our wedding had he not gone back to Wisconsin.

"Yes," I said, my tone guarded. "He's back in town. He was with me today when I talked to Julie."

"So are you two..."

"No."

She let out a loud sigh. "Why ever not? This is truly ridiculous, Daphne."

"Honestly, Mom? I don't know. I could swear he still has feelings for me. But he said we only went out a few times, and that he's not looking for more. His words don't really match his actions. But maybe he's just a nice guy who can't help but play the knight in shining armor." I let out a deep sigh of my own.

"So is it truly over then?"

"I don't know. He acts like it is, but..."

My gut told me that no matter what Emerson was acting like right now, it wasn't the end of the story.

I couldn't help but smile, knowing that my gut was usually right.

As I drove the winding mountain road back home, I mulled over everything that had happened that day. I was excited—more excited and inspired than I had felt in a long time, frankly. I wasn't sure what that said about me. The last investigation had ended with not one, but two attempts on my life. My brain kept telling me to just stay out of all of it.

But my gut? That was a different story.

I felt like I could help, and more than that, I *wanted* to be involved. Even if it turned out that the journal had nothing to do with Eileen.

The truth was that my photo editing work had stopped feeding my soul a long time ago. At first, I had loved it. I was good at it, and I loved being an independent entrepreneur who could work from anywhere. I was proud of the galleries I delivered to my clients.

But what had once felt so exciting and fulfilling had started to feel like, well, just a job. That change happened when Dad got sick, and I had assumed it was because I was overwhelmed with his care and already grieving the inevitable loss.

But even after turning the corner on that grief, the joy of my work had never come back.

Even my coffee-table book project wasn't as exciting as it should have been.

But this?

A treasure hunt was downright thrilling. And as much as I hated to admit it, I felt a little thrill about helping with the murder investigation as well.

Something about it made me feel more alive.

WITHOUT THINKING TWICE, I turned my car into Fiona's driveway instead of going straight home. Her house was just before mine, a short walk on a nice day. But I was so eager to talk to her that I didn't want to wait the extra five minutes.

She swung her front door open before I even got out of my car. Fiona swore she didn't have the sight, but she always seemed to know when I was coming. It was impossible to catch her by surprise. The only time I had ever shocked her was the day I had moved in. She had walked over with an apple pie to meet me. I opened the door, and she dropped the plate in shock, thinking she was seeing my mother.

But since then, she had always been a step ahead of me.

"Come on in, Daphne," she called out with a wave. "I have the teakettle going. Come in and sit a spell."

I stopped to embrace her before slipping off my boots and walking into her house. She was always barefoot indoors, and I liked to follow suit.

Her cottage was the most charming place on earth, as far as I was concerned. Tiny and cozy, it seemed to glow with magic. Botanical prints hung on every wall. The living room always felt so welcoming with a fire going in the fireplace. Her furniture was cozy and just begging to be curled up in. Her kitchen felt like stepping into a storybook, with jars of dried herbs lining the open shelving, lavender and garlic braids strung from the ceiling, and stacks of mismatched teacups ready to go for company. She was always making tea for her guests, creating formulas on the spot that seemed to be exactly what you needed, no matter what you were feeling.

I asked her once, teasingly, if she was a witch. She had replied mildly, "Of course not, dear. I'm Irish."

I followed Fiona into her kitchen and sat down at her table, taking off my layers in the warmth.

She looked me over appraisingly. "Well. There's the brightness I've been looking for. Whatever happened to make you feel better? You and Emerson patch things up and take a little roll in the hay, did ya?"

I blushed. "Fiona! Of course not."

"That's a shame," she said, tongue clucking. "I thought for sure if I had him drive you home, you two would figure things out."

I shook my head and chuckled despite myself. "I'm afraid not. But I have other news." I caught her up to speed on everything as she mixed up one of her tea formulas and steeped us each a cup, mixed with the wildflower honey she collected herself.

"Well, my, my. A treasure hunt! Now that's a bit of excitement, isn't it? Now I see what's pinking up your cheeks and brightening your eyes. You've got another case to solve." She walked to the table and placed the teacup down, looking at me fondly. "You really are just like your mama."

That familiar ache came back. "I still wish I could have known her."

"I know. That's why I always point it out when I see her in you. That way, you can at least know her a bit through yourself. And she would have been just as excited as you to have found out something like this."

"That was one thing I wanted to ask you. Do you think she did? I have to say, I'm wondering if that's the journal from the vision. If she found out about a treasure and was hunting for it, and if someone else found out…"

Fiona frowned. "I see what you mean. Whatever was troubling her before she died, she never told me. And she never told me anything about treasure either. But knowing her, I don't think a treasure hunt would have made her anxious and worried the way she was there at the end. I think she would have looked exactly like you look now. Like a hound dog who just caught a whiff of a rabbit and can't wait to go chasing after it."

I laughed. "Maybe you're right. Maybe they aren't connected at all. And yeah, maybe I'm just excited about trying to figure this out."

"So," she leaned forward, eyes sparkling. "When do we start?"

"We?" I asked, bemused.

"Daphne Sullivan, you aren't going searching for gold on these mountains without me. You wouldn't leave a poor old woman out of the last fun she might have in this life, now would you?"

I rolled my eyes, unable to keep the grin off my face. Fiona's life was way more fascinating and challenging than my own.

"Besides," she continued, taking a sip of her tea. "We both know if you went without me, you wouldn't get more than twenty feet deep in the woods before you tucked tail and headed back to your car, thinking you heard a bear after you."

Well. She had a point there.

Chapter Thirteen

Daphne

Fiona and I finished our tea, then headed straight back into town for a visit to the local library. I had never been there, but Fiona suggested it might be a good place to research Della Porter, and I agreed. Plus, whether or not we actually found anything, it felt great to be doing something. Everything in my life had felt stagnant for weeks. Finally taking action felt fantastic.

Rosemary Mountain Public Library was in an older part of town, surrounded by shade trees and mid-century houses. It didn't appear to have been updated in quite some time, which made me instantly fall in love. Of course, I had never met a library I didn't adore. Still, this one felt special, like a moment frozen in time. It had the deep smell of old books, with worn-out chairs beside inexpensive tables lit by dated gold floor lamps. It was just a little too dark, a bit too dusty, and could probably use a thorough cleaning.

It was amazing.

There were two librarians at the front, complete opposites in every way. The older—and senior ranking, made obvious by her body language—was the most cliché librarian I had ever seen in my life. Her hair was pulled back in a severe bun. She wore black-rimmed glasses on a chain, a high-necked blouse buttoned all the way to the top, and a heavy gray sweater. She frowned the moment we walked in, looking down her nose at us.

"Fiona," she said with a slight nod, her tone frosty.

"Hello, Iris," Fiona replied, her tone colder than I had ever heard it.

The other librarian jumped to greet us. He was much younger than Iris—probably not much older than me—with a friendly face. Like her, he wore glasses, and he also had a sweater over his black button-down shirt. But the similarities ended there. He seemed delighted to see us. His face absolutely lit up as he walked over to welcome us.

"Welcome to our library," he said, pumping my hand. "I'm Jasper McMillan. I've heard about you, of course, but I'm glad you finally stopped in to see us. It's good to see you again, Fiona." He shook her hand as well, grinning from ear to ear. Iris huffed in the background. "What can I do for you ladies today?"

I had to stifle a giggle. He reminded me of a server in a restaurant, eager to earn a big tip. I wasn't used to personal service at a library.

"Actually, we're here to do some research. We're trying to learn more about a lady who may have lived here in the early 1900s. Della Porter."

"Oh." His face paled. "This must be about that poor man on the news."

"Now, how did you know that?" Fiona asked.

"He was in here asking about the same woman just a few days before his body was found," Jasper told us, his eyes darting back and forth.

Fiona and I exchanged glances. I knew from talking to Julie that Wes had asked for help from a librarian, but I decided to play dumb to see what we could find out.

"Was he really? Can you tell me more about that?" I asked.

Iris stepped in. "Jasper, may I remind you that we always respect our patrons' privacy?" She set her lips in a thin line and glared at him above her glasses.

"Oh, yes, of course," he stammered. His face went from pale to as red as the hair on his head. I felt sorry for him working for such a woman.

She raised an eyebrow and went back to her work, attempting to appear as if she was ignoring us. But it was obvious she was keeping an ear open.

"Well, I suppose I can't tell you about poor Mr. Adams," Jasper began hesitantly. "But, of course, I can help you in your research regarding Della Porter."

"We would really appreciate that." I smiled at him warmly.

"Why don't you ladies have a seat over there, and I will be right with you." He gestured at the table farthest from Iris with a slight bow. I was once again reminded of a server.

"Thank you," Fiona said politely, with a small glare toward Iris. I had to stifle another laugh.

"What the heck, Fiona? What's with you and Iris?" I whispered as we made our way to the table to wait for Jasper.

Fiona's nostrils flared. "That woman is a two-timing, man-stealing, piece of—well, I can't say what of. But you get the picture."

"Well, okay then." I shook my head, lost for words, and took a seat at the table to study Iris from across the room. It was hard to reconcile the prim and proper woman behind the desk with what Fiona said. I had to assume that their fight went way, way back, because I couldn't imagine Iris stealing any men for at least the last two decades.

"Ah, ladies, thank you for waiting." Jasper slid into the chair beside me, straightening his tie. He placed some papers on the table in front of us.

"This is the same information I shared with Mr. Adams," he said, his voice low, with a glance toward Iris. "He was interested in Della Porter's records and genealogy. As you can see, Ms. Porter lived in the area from roughly 1880 until her death in 1904. She was known to be, ahem, a *lady of the night,* living in a downtown brothel until 1902, when she apparently saved up enough money to buy a place of her own. She moved to what we now call Lonely Oak Road and set up house there until her death."

Fiona and I looked at each other. I was certain my eyes were as big as hers.

"How would a, um, *lady of the night,* as you said, be able to save up that kind of money? Was that common?" I asked.

He bowed his head again. "Forgive me, for I am a librarian, not a historian. But I do read a lot," he said, grinning. "My understanding from reading Tennessee history is that roughly one in ten women in that profession were able to be upwardly mobile. Typically, that would occur from either becoming a 'madame' in charge, or by making, um, friends with the elite men in society, or from offering a wide range of services."

My eyes must have widened at the last one, because he jumped in to clarify. "Wide range, as in also offering alcohol or fortune telling services, or even, I'm afraid to say, drugs such as morphine."

"I see," I said. "So it wasn't common, but it also wasn't unheard of for a woman to make some serious money?"

"Not unheard of, no."

I decided to push for a little more. "Jasper, did Mr. Adams ask you anything else? Or did he tell you anything about why he was researching this woman?"

Jasper hesitated, immediately looking toward Iris. Her back was to us, thankfully.

"He didn't really ask many questions; he just wanted all the research I could help him find. He was nice, but not particularly talkative. The other man, though..." Jasper shuddered as he trailed off.

"What other man?" My heart raced.

"He was with another man. Real brute of a guy. I swear, he looked at me like he would rip my tongue out just for speaking."

"Well, who was it?" Fiona popped in.

Jasper shook his head quickly and shrugged. "I don't know. Not local. I had never seen him before. I can describe him for you. He was huge. At least six foot two and built like a tank. His head was shaved, but he had a beard. That's all I noticed. I tried not to look at him too much." He shuddered again.

"Jasper, do you have security cameras? We need to tell the police this."

His jaw dropped. "The police? But why?"

For a librarian who knew a lot of history, he sure didn't seem to be all that sharp.

"Because that man could have been the last person to see Mr. Adams alive. He could be the number one suspect."

"Suspect? Do you mean Mr. Adams was *murdered*?"

"Didn't you know?"

"No." Jasper's face went paler than I could have imagined possible. "The news just said a hiker was found dead on Hidden Lake Trail. Later, they identified it as him, and I remembered him being here. I assumed he had some sort of accident on the trail. I thought it was because of—" he clamped his mouth shut.

"Because of what?"

He glanced around frantically before leaning forward to speak again.

"Because of the *curse.*"

Chapter Fourteen

Daphne

"What curse?" My heart pounded as my mind raced with possibilities. First a lost treasure, now a curse?

Without answering me, Jasper got up and hurried over to a book-shelf, apparently looking for something. I looked at Fiona, who shrugged.

He came back and thrust a book into my hands.

"The story is in there," he said. "That's a book of local history. Back when Rosemary Mountain was first founded—before Tennessee was even a state—the settlement was, of course, harsh by our standards. Crime wasn't tolerated, and punishments were quite brutal. As it happened, the governor at the time was expecting his first child. The child was stillborn. He was quite upset about it and blamed the midwife for negligence."

At this, Fiona—a midwife herself—let out a loud harrumph.

"Anyway," Jasper went on, with a quick glance her way. "They sentenced the midwife to be whipped and cropped—"

"Cropped?" I interrupted, unfamiliar with the term.

"A barbaric practice, I'm afraid," he said apologetically. "After her whipping, they nailed her ears to the pillory for an hour. Her ears were then, ahem, removed from her head in order to free her when her punishment was up. Unfortunately, the midwife was pregnant herself. She miscarried the night after her punishment and was beside herself with grief and rage."

"I would imagine so," I said. "That's absolutely horrific."

He bowed his head again. "She was apparently never the same after. She burned down the governor's house with him in it, then tried to run away, using that very trail. When the townsmen caught up to her, she told them that the place was cursed and that if they dared lay a hand on her head, she would kill them, too. She jumped into the creek, which was swollen and raging at the time. Her body was found washed up on the bank two days later."

My eyes must have been as wide as saucers.

"Ever since then, people have heard wailing on the mountain, and some say they've spotted her walking the trail, looking for the soul of her lost baby. There's also a long history of men dying on that trail," Jasper continued, tapping the top of the book with his long finger. "It's all in there. So when I saw the news, I figured, well, it must be her, still seeking her revenge."

"Hogwash," Fiona said loudly.

Iris immediately began walking our way, heels clipping, her eyes narrowed at Fiona.

"I've been up on that trail a million times," Fiona continued, not bothering to lower her voice. "And I've always been just fine. This whole curse idea is just plain nonsense."

"Yes, but you are a woman," Jasper said gently. "I would never dare to go up that trail, and I can tell you that there are a lot of men in this town who feel the same way, whether or not they'll admit it. Bad things happen to men on that mountain." He shivered, and I found myself doing the same.

Fiona just rolled her eyes.

Iris reached the table and placed both her hands on it, leaning toward Fiona.

"May I remind you that this is a public space, and that you are expected to remain quiet?"

Fiona stood up and placed her own hands on the table. "And may I remind *you* that—"

"Sorry," I interrupted, grabbing Fiona's arm. "We were just wrapping up. Thank you for the history lesson, Jasper. I'd like to set up a library card so I can check out this book."

"My pleasure." He grinned and gave me a little wink as we both guided Fiona away from the table.

"You should have let me finish," Fiona grumbled.

"Maybe next time," I whispered back. "But we may need to come back here for more information, so keep it together."

She huffed again. "You get your library card. I'm going to wait outside on the bench." She tossed her long braid behind her and practically flounced out of the building.

"She's quite the character," Jasper chuckled.

"She is." I grinned. "I love her to death. I've never seen her so riled up."

"It's like that every time she comes in." He glanced around to make sure Iris couldn't hear us. "I have to admit, I sort of enjoy watching her give Iris a hard time."

"Me too," I whispered conspiratorially. "It seems like she's a difficult person to work for."

He shrugged. "Every job has its pros and cons, as they say. I get to be here surrounded by books all day and actually earn a living doing it. She's a small price to pay for that."

"That's a good way to look at it."

"I think so," he said with a grin. "Now just fill out this card with your information and let me see your driver's license, and you'll be good to go. I'll put this in a bag for you."

He wrapped the old book in tissue paper and placed it into a bag, reminding me again of a server instead of a librarian. But despite his quirks, I liked the guy. He was friendly and interesting. He was even sort of cute, in a nerdy kind of way. *But he's not Emerson.* I sighed. Why did Emerson always have to invade my thoughts?

Jasper returned with my bag, then took my information and entered it into the computer. He scanned a library card, then handed it to me. "Here you go. Looks like everything is in order. I put that book on your account. It's due in two weeks, but you can always call to renew it if you need longer. Also, I put my card in there. Please feel free to call me if I can answer any more questions for you." He blushed, and I couldn't help but feel flattered.

"Thanks," I said, returning his smile. "I'll do that. I appreciate all your help today. I learned a lot."

He blushed again and made that funny little bow.

I smiled and said goodbye. As I walked toward the door, I vowed to put all thoughts of Emerson Jones out of my mind for good.

Chapter Fifteen

My fist slammed into the punching bag, sending it swinging.

It felt good.

"Whoa, man. What's got your panties in a wad?" Greg smirked at me, tossing me a towel.

I wiped the sweat from my forehead, then grabbed my water bottle and gulped greedily. "What do you think?"

"I'm guessing it has something to do with a certain green-eyed, red-headed, stubborn-ass woman," he said with a chuckle. "What's wrong? You two having a fight about something?"

I scowled and went back to the bag. "No. I ended things."

Greg blinked.

"Say what?"

"I broke things off while I was in Wisconsin."

Greg walked over to me, his eyes showing concern. "What in the world for? I mean, I know I was the one telling you to break up with her before that. But I was wrong about her, and I'm man enough to admit it. After everything else, what on earth could have made you end it?"

I punched the bag again. Hard. "You wouldn't understand."

"Why don't you try me?"

I looked over at Greg and sighed. He was a good man and a good friend. Not quite a father figure—the age difference between us was just low enough to keep us in the buddy realm. But I had a hell of a lot of respect for him just the same.

I walked over to the folding chairs and plopped into one, taking another swig of water. "It's about my brother."

Greg blinked hard. "Alex? What does he have to do with it? He do some in-depth background check on her or something, dig something up?"

"Not Alex. Ken."

It hurt to say the name. Other than Doc Rogers, Daphne was the only one I had spoken that name to since the day I moved to Rosemary Mountain.

Greg frowned and came to sit by me. "I guess I haven't heard you talk about Ken. What's the problem there?"

"Ken was my baby brother. He got killed in Afghanistan a few years back."

Greg was quiet for a moment. "I'm sorry man, I didn't know. But I guess I don't understand what that has to do with Daphne."

It hurt, thinking of it all. Hurt so bad I didn't know if I could even say it. I had never said any of this out loud, just carried it, kept it all stuffed down. Wasn't sure what would happen if I started letting it up.

"I've got my reasons. That's all."

"Alright." Greg wasn't the kind of man to push. "But I think you're an idiot."

I snorted.

"I mean it," he continued. "I've known you for, what, two years now? You were the happiest I've ever seen you when you were with Daphne. So whatever's going on, yeah. I think you're an idiot. It's plain to see you're still hung up on her. Otherwise, you wouldn't be trying to destroy county property over there."

"Sorry about that," I muttered. "Look, it's over, okay? It's not going to happen. But then I ran into her this morning. Of course, she's investigating again. Putting herself in danger. So I got involved. Then I saw her and Detective Ford together, and well, I just needed to take out some frustration. That's all. I'll be back to normal in no time."

"What do you mean you saw her and Detective Ford together?" Greg seemed to be fighting back a smile.

"When he responded to the scene at the motel. He grinned when he saw her. It's obvious they're buddies already. Which is good. He can look out for her." I was trying very hard to keep any hint of bitterness out of my voice, but I wasn't sure I was succeeding.

"Interesting." Greg's face remained strained, like if he didn't fight against it, he would break out into a grin. "Well, Jackson's a good guy, no doubt about it. And I have to admit, I've developed a fondness for Daphne, even if she seems to have a way of getting in the middle of things. I suppose there are worse things than them becoming *buddies*."

"Yep." I got up and walked back over to the punching bag, giving it a few more hard hits.

"Well, you enjoy taking your frustration out on that bag there. I suppose I should thank you for choosing a positive way to let off steam compared to some of our residents here." He grinned. "I'm heading back to my office. Going to get a report from Detective Ford." The grin widened.

I hit the bag even harder.

I could hear him laughing all the way down the hall.

AFTER MY WORKOUT, I grabbed a quick shower right there at the station. Using their gym was one of the perks of being friends with the sheriff. I usually worked out at the life flight base unless Greg and I were training together, but I hadn't wanted to drive all the way out there for an impromptu workout on a day when I had other errands to run in town.

And I was avoiding my normal off-day runs, because I knew if I started running on our road, there was a good chance I would run straight to Daphne's door.

After I was cleaned up and thinking straight again, I left the station to run my errands. I was determined not to think about Daphne and "Jackson."

I wasn't successful.

It felt like everywhere I went in Rosemary Mountain was a reminder of her. What I needed was a distraction. Something to keep my mind busy. Maybe this was the perfect time to start reading again.

With that, I turned my truck toward the library.

As I WALKED up the sidewalk toward the library entrance, I spotted Fiona sitting alone outside on a bench. I almost groaned. If Fiona was here, then there was a good chance Daphne was too. Thankfully, she was nowhere in sight.

"Hey, Fiona," I said, waving. She was a character for sure, maybe even a little crazy. But I couldn't help liking her.

"Oh, Emerson," she said, holding out a trembling hand. "Come sit with me a moment, won't you?"

Something about her voice seemed off, feeble almost. She *was* old. I usually forgot it, because she always seemed so vibrant. But today, her age was showing.

I sat beside her, and she placed a shaky hand on my arm.

"I'm so glad I saw you," she said, her voice still weak. "I don't want to be a bother, but, well, I'm afraid I just can't do everything I used to. I got some firewood delivered this week, but the man who dropped it off just dumped it by the road. Do you think you could come help me stack it on the porch, so I can get to it easier when winter comes?"

"Of course," I said. "That's what neighbors are for, right?"

"Oh, thank you," she said, patting me softly. "I'll pay you for your time, of course."

"Oh, no," I protested. "I really don't mind stacking it for you. I couldn't accept any money."

"Well, then, I'll cook you a nice dinner as a thank you."

I protested again, but she cut me off.

"That'll be as much a treat for me as a thank you for you. You know, I'm so lonely, not having any family of my own." Her voice got even more feeble and sad. "Sometimes it's just so hard being out there alone with no one to talk to."

"Dinner would be lovely," I said, gently. "What time would you like me to come?" Poor woman. She was really declining rapidly, but sometimes that happened. It was always sad to see someone so vibrant fade. The least I could do was give her some company and some help.

"Let's say about four-thirty. Come then, stack the wood, and I'll have dinner ready after."

"That sounds perfect. I'll be there."

"Oh, bless you, Emerson," she cooed, patting my hand.

A nearby voice interrupted. "And what are we blessing him for?"

I closed my eyes and drew in a deep breath. *Daphne.*

"He's going to help me with some chores, sweet man," Fiona explained, still patting my hand.

Daphne gave her an odd look.

"Well, that's nice of you, Emerson." She glanced my way and threw me a smile.

I wanted to grab onto it and save it for a rainy day.

"Are you ready, Fiona?" she asked. "I'm all set."

"Oh, yes, dear." Fiona got up, her back hunched, and grabbed onto Daphne's arm. "So sweet of you to bring me out for some company. Goodbye, Emerson, and thank you again."

"Goodbye, Fiona."

Daphne gave me a half smile, and I returned it, despite myself. She and Fiona headed toward the parking lot, and I turned reluctantly back toward the library, knowing that no book was going to stop me from thinking of Daphne's green eyes tonight.

Chapter Sixteen

Daphne

Fiona clung to my arm as we walked toward her truck.

"Did you sprain your ankle or something? What's wrong?" I looked her over, trying to figure out what had happened in the few minutes I was in the library.

She looked back behind us, then straightened up. "My ankle. Yes, maybe that's what it was. But I'm feeling much better now. Thank you, dear." She patted my arm and started walking normally.

I laughed. "That was a fast recovery. Anyway, I got the book, and Jasper gave me his number in case we have any more questions about the curse."

Fiona frowned as we climbed into her truck. "I'm telling you there is no curse. What utter nonsense."

I was taken aback. "I'm kind of surprised to hear you say that, Fiona."

"Why, dear?"

"Well, because you're the most mystical, superstitious person I've ever met. I would think if anyone believed in curses, it would be you."

She waved a hand in dismissal. "Do curses exist? Probably. But the only wailing I've heard on that mountain was from babies and birthing mamas. Well, and one bobcat. And as far as men dying on that trail, remember, I've lived here for longer than I'd like to admit. I've been here for some of those. Are you telling me a *curse* made Jim Bob die when he was stupid enough to go hiking so drunk that he thought a black bear was his woman and tried to snuggle up with it? Was it a *curse* that killed old Andy when he camped out in the rain, used his cook stove inside his tent without ventilating it, and poisoned himself with carbon monoxide?"

Oh, she was fired up now.

"Well, no, those things sound like stupidity," I admitted.

"Exactly. But no, let's blame a long-dead *woman* for it instead."

I smiled at her. "When you put it that way, I see what you mean."

"Changing the subject," she said. "Before I forget, can you come over for dinner tomorrow night? Around five-thirty?"

"Sure. Any special occasion?"

"Not at all," she said with a little grin. "I'm just in the mood for some company, that's all."

AFTER PARTING WAYS WITH FIONA, I shot Jackson a quick text that I might have come across some helpful information. He replied that he was in a meeting, but would get back with me. So, I reluctantly spent the next few hours getting some work done. It felt like a drudge, but it was necessary.

The truth was that my financial burdens were really starting to scare me. It was amazing how quickly that had happened. Only a few months ago, I had felt financially secure. I had a thriving business, plus I had inherited the house and some life insurance from my dad. I had actually paid cash for my cottage and felt sure I was making good financial decisions and could support myself.

I hadn't realized just how many medical bills there were to pay. Or how much my dad had really spent on his collections. It was downright shocking how big a spender he was, and how very little he had in savings.

Now, there wasn't any money left, and his mortgage and home maintenance costs were hanging over my head each month. That, combined with losing my best-paying clients, and financial security felt a million miles away.

So, drudgery or not, I needed to put in the work to rebuild my business and bring in some cash.

Just as I was feeling like I couldn't work for even one more minute, I heard a knock. Butterflies danced in my stomach as my mind instantly turned to Emerson. It wouldn't be the first time he had knocked on my door to reconnect.

With a little wave of anticipation, I opened the door. Instead of Emerson, I found Jackson standing there. Only this time, he wasn't grinning.

"Hey, come on in," I said. "But you could have just called me. You didn't have to drive all the way out here. What I found out isn't really that big."

"Nah, it's fine. I needed to talk to you anyway."

Anticipation turned to a wave of anxiety.

"Okay. Have a seat wherever," I said, gesturing to my living room. "Can I get you something to drink?"

"No, but thanks." He took a seat on the brown leather sofa and leaned forward, his elbows on his knees.

I sat nervously in the corner chair, waiting for him to speak.

"You go first," he said.

"Okay." I caught him up on mine and Fiona's trip to the library and what we had learned there. His eyes lit up, and he took careful notes.

"That really is interesting," he said. "I'll have to talk to them and see if I can figure out who this other man was with Mr. Adams. Great work, Daphne."

I blushed with pleasure. "Your turn."

He let out a sigh. "I've been talking with Bill Brinksley. He asked me to look into something."

"Oh yeah? I know Julie said they had asked permission to search on his land."

"Yeah. That's why I went to interview him as soon as I finished with her. Apparently, Wes and Julie had good reason to believe the treasure was somewhere on his property. But they didn't find it there. And now, Bill has decided that's because your father found it first."

"My father?" I was a little confused.

"Your dad's name was Lonnie Sullivan, right?"

"Right."

"Yeah. So Bill says that Lonnie kept trespassing on his property, searching for something. Bill didn't know what it was at the time, but he kept telling Lonnie to stay off his land. When all this happened, he remembered what had happened back then. Has it in his mind that Lonnie was looking for the treasure and found it, and that's why he and Mr. Adams couldn't."

"But that's crazy." *Was it, though? Didn't that sound just like Dad?* "I guess I'm still missing something. Why would he be asking you to look into it now?"

Jackson sighed. "Legal precedent here in Tennessee is that if a treasure trove is found, it legally belongs to whoever's property it was found on."

"I see. So that's why Bill was so willing to let Wes and Julie search on his land." That made sense now.

"Exactly," Jackson confirmed. "He thought that if they found the treasure, he would have the rights to it. He didn't tell them that, of course. But that's what he was thinking. And now he has his heart set on that treasure. Since he thinks Lonnie found it, well, you should prepare yourself for potential legal trouble. And financial trouble, if we're being honest."

I closed my eyes and let out an exhale. "You're saying if Dad found it on Bill's land, Bill might still have a right to it. And he's definitely the kind of guy who would take me to court."

Jackson nodded. "I'm afraid so. I'm not a lawyer, and obviously, I've never dealt with a situation like this before. I don't know how the courts might handle that. I don't know if he can prove Lonnie found it at all, much less that it was found on his land. But I just thought you should have a heads up that he's making moves that way."

"I appreciate it. I'm just sort of stunned right now." This was all just unbelievable.

"I'm afraid there's more."

My heart sank. "More? Seriously?"

He nodded. "If Lonnie found it, and anyone can prove that, there might be other issues. Because even if it was found on *Lonnie's* land, the treasure trove rulings might not apply. Again, I'm not a lawyer," he said, holding up his hands. "But my understanding is that for a find to be considered a treasure, the owner has to be unknown. In this situation, with the journals, we know who the original owner was. There could be legitimate heirs. I just don't know. It's a complicated one."

"So what you're saying is, odds are, if Dad found the money, I'm going to have to pay it back." I shook my head in disbelief.

"I'd say that's a good possibility."

"How much are we talking?"

He cleared his throat. "Well, according to Julie, they thought they were looking for sixty thousand in gold coins. That's sixty thousand back in 1900. Adjusting for inflation, that would be worth about two million today."

My jaw hit the floor. "Two million dollars? You've got to be kidding me. Even if I sold everything I own, there's no way it would come close to that."

"I understand," he said gently. "We'll figure this out. I just wanted you to hear it from me before Bill harasses you."

"Thank you. Really." I shook my head in disbelief.

I was starting to think that moving here had been the worst mistake of my life.

Chapter Seventeen

It was a gorgeous day, warm for this time of year, and I felt on edge. So edgy that I would have volunteered for an extra shift at work, except for my promise to help Fiona stack her firewood.

I tried to stay busy on my own. Took the dog for a walk through the woods, gave the chickens some extra attention, and caught up on some of the outdoor chores that had gone undone while I was away. I had paid a friend to take care of things while I was gone, but that wasn't the same as being here myself, and there was plenty to catch up on. Even so, by late afternoon, I knew I needed to find something to distract me.

It was Ken's birthday, a day I dreaded every year.

A day when I didn't need to be alone with my thoughts.

So I headed over to Fiona's earlier than planned. I figured she could put me to work doing some extra chores. Poor woman seemed to have aged ten years in just a few days.

I knocked on her door and heard her calling from inside in a singsong voice. "Hold your horses, I'll be there in a minute!"

It was probably taking her longer to get around these days.

After a couple of minutes, the door swung open.

"Oh! Emerson!" Fiona's face was all surprise.

So was mine, for that matter. Because the woman standing in front of me wasn't stooped over like yesterday, nor was her voice weak. In fact, she was practically glowing. She was wearing her signature overalls, and her long white hair was tied up in a messy bun, like someone less than half her age would do. Her hands were stained purple, like she was hard at work doing something that required at least a little strength.

The woman had tricked me. Of course.

Fiona Flanagan would never grow old and feeble. She was too damn stubborn.

"Hello, Fiona," I said, my mouth twitching.

"Well, Emerson, dear, come on in," she said in that old lady voice she had used yesterday, dropping her shoulders into a stoop.

"You can cut the act," I said dryly. "I'll still stack your firewood."

She let out a loud laugh. "Well, I guess you caught me. Sorry about that. But I really *did* want some company today, and the old lady card always works like a charm."

"It's okay." I smiled, and it warmed me from the inside. "Truth be told, I could use some company today too. I'm glad you tricked me."

Her eyes peered at me sharply, and I got the feeling she could see right through to my very soul. I wouldn't doubt it. I normally didn't believe in such things, but with Fiona, anything seemed possible.

"Tell you what," she said. "Why don't you get started on that firewood? I get the feeling you're just itching for something physical to do today. I'm almost done making my elderberry syrup, then I need to put on our dinner. I'll wrap up in the kitchen and then bring us both out a cup of tea, okay? We can sit a spell on the porch together."

I nodded. "Sounds like a plan."

I pulled my work gloves out of my pocket and started moving wood. Whoever delivered it had just dumped it all at the end of her driveway. Pretty poor customer service, especially for an elderly lady. And some of it was too big for her fireplace. I set those aside, knowing I would need to come back with an ax to split them. But there were enough decent pieces to create a nice stack on her front porch and to start refilling her woodshed.

It felt good to do something to make her life a little easier.

. . .

After a bit, she came out and called to tell me that tea was ready. I brought a few more logs with me to the porch, then took off my gloves and sat down in the rocker next to her. She handed me a cup and I took a long sip. The flavor was surprising, unlike anything I had tasted before.

"What is this?" I asked.

"Oh, a little of this, a little of that. One of my own recipes." She paused for a minute. "I added some Hawthorn berries to it today. Hawthorn is good for your heart."

"Is it now?" I asked, a little amused. I knew Fiona believed strongly in using plants for medicine. As an RN, I found the whole thing a little silly, but figured it was probably harmless as long as she didn't convince people to avoid real medicine in favor of her 'remedies.'

"Yes," she said, her voice serious. "Funny thing about Hawthorn. Studies have found it to be cardio-protective. It increases coronary artery blood flow, lowers blood pressure, reduces inflammation..."

"Really?" I found myself interested, despite my reservations about using herbs as medicine.

"Really. But the funny thing is that it doesn't just work on the physical heart. It's a powerful herb for heartbreak as well. It's one I always turn to when someone is struggling with grief. Or guilt."

I stared at her. "How did you know?"

"Oh, son, it's written all over you." She placed her own teacup gently on the table between us. "Now, why don't you tell old Fiona what's troubling you?"

I took another long sip of the tea. Funny, I had always thought her 'medicine' was a joke. Now, I wasn't so sure. Something in me seemed to be moving, shifting. And instead of wanting to bury everything about Ken even deeper, I found myself wanting to confide in her. To finally let it out.

"Today's my brother's birthday," I said, looking down at my cup. I took another sip, hoping it might give me some courage as well. "He would have been twenty-six."

Fiona sat quietly, giving me the space I needed to find the words.

"He idolized me," I said. "Followed me around. Wanted to be just like me. We were close. My other brother, Alex, was always on a different track than me and Ken. Alex is a real nerd." I snorted. "Ken and I were the wild ones. Always getting into trouble. Anyway. I joined the Air Force as a medic. When I joined, of course, Ken had to join the military too. And, because he needed to one-up me, he became a Marine."

"Tough job," Fiona commented.

"Yep. Sure was. Long story short, we ended up on tour in Afghanistan at the same time. I was wrapping up my deployment when he got there. He was all excited. It was his first tour, and he wanted to prove himself."

Fiona lifted her teapot and poured me another cup. I drank it, grateful for a chance to pause for a moment. Finally, I spoke again.

"He was killed his first week there." The pain of it hit me as hard as ever.

"I'm sorry," she said softly.

"IED," I continued when I found my voice again. "He was still alive when they brought him into the hospital. I was there. I couldn't save him."

The images flashed through my mind, a nightmare from which I could never escape.

Fiona reached over and patted my arm while I tried to find my voice again. Tried to block out the images I couldn't bear to see.

"It was my fault," I said, fighting to get out the last of it. "He never would have joined if I hadn't. He had dreams. Big ones. He was smart. Could have done so many things. Had a fiancée back home. They were planning on getting married when he finished his tour. He always wanted to be a dad."

My voice broke, and I couldn't continue.

"Emerson." Fiona's voice broke through the fog. "It wasn't your fault. He made his own decisions. Sometimes things happen, and we can't find a reason why. But blaming yourself isn't the answer."

"I should have known," I choked out. "When I joined, I should have known he would follow suit. And of course, he would have to go the more dangerous route. You know, all the branches make fun of the Air Force, and while it sucks, the truth is that my job was cushy compared to his." I shook my head. "It should have been me. I'm the one who wanted to serve. He should have stayed home, married his girl, had lots of babies, and lived his life. I should have been the one to die in that hellhole."

"Survivor's guilt," Fiona said. "What you're feeling is normal. But normal doesn't mean true." She took a long sip of tea herself and sighed. "I don't know why bad things happen. I wish I did. I wish your brother had never died, and that you never had to bear this. But this is the way things are. And I may not have known your brother, but I know this. If he loved you, and I know he did, then he wouldn't want you to keep suffering over something you can't change."

"I made him a promise," I said, staring off at the trees swaying in the wind. "When he was lying there. Dying. I made him a promise."

"What promise was that?"

"He was crying out for Sarah. His girl. He was out of his head, thinking she was there. Apologizing to her for dying, for not being able to marry her and give her the kids they had dreamed of. I promised to take care of her, and I promised him I would never get married or have kids either."

"Oh, Emerson." Fiona let out a deep sigh. "Is that why you never looked at a single girl in Rosemary Mountain until Daphne arrived, and then you broke up with her before you two even really got started?"

I nodded.

"Your brother wouldn't want that for you. You know that, deep down."

"I screwed up when I asked Daphne out. She got here, and I met her, and... I don't know, Fiona." I ran a hand through my hair in frustration. "When I saw her in the fish house that night, I saw something in her eyes that made me feel like she might understand how broken I was. Because she seemed broken and scared, too. And I hadn't been home in so long that there was starting to be a little space between me and Ken, you know?"

"Yeah, I know what you mean."

"I thought maybe it would be okay for me to be happy." That thought hurt, even now. "Then I went back home. After losing Ken, Mom panicked when she heard what happened to me here. She needed to see me, to see that I was really okay. But I saw Sarah too. And Ken's memorial. And it all just came back. I realized how damn selfish I was to think I could just run away from it and find some happiness."

Fiona patted my hand again. "You've got a burden on you, for sure. But I hope you'll find a way to put that burden down. It's not yours to carry."

"I never break a promise," I said, my face set.

She sighed and turned her own gaze to the forest. "I understand. But if I make you up a bag of dried tea, will you keep drinking it?"

I gave her a half smile. "You know, I think I will."

"Good. Son, your heart needs some healing. And I know you're set on keeping your promise, but how do you feel about being friends with Daphne?"

I stared down at my empty tea cup. "I want to be her friend, but right now? It's really hard to be around her. She deserves to move on and find happiness, but it's painful to watch. It's painful to see her and feel drawn to her, knowing I can't have her. I've never felt as drawn to anyone as I am to her. I can't even explain it. She's not even my type." I gave a small laugh, rubbing my hand over my weary eyes. "But there's something about her. I feel things for her I don't have any right to feel."

Fiona sighed again. "Well, Emerson, I'm afraid I have a confession to make."

"What's that?"

"I sort of invited her over for dinner, and"—she checked her watch — "she'll be here any minute."

Chapter Eighteen

Daphne

I was relieved when it was finally time to go to Fiona's for dinner. I had forced myself to stay home and focus on work all day, even though all I wanted was to dig into the book Jasper had recommended about the history of Rosemary Mountain. The curse was intriguing, and the idea of finding buried treasure was just so tantalizing. But Jackson's news about potential legal trouble had at least lit a fire under me as far as work went. I finished every outstanding project on my list and reached out to three new photographers about my services.

It was a good, productive day. But man, I was glad it was done.

I bundled up in my coat and briefly considered walking to Fiona's. It was such a beautiful day. But the sun was already getting low, and it would be pitch black by the time I returned. Her house was the one closest to mine, a short walk the length of a city block or two. Even so, I would take my car, though it made me feel silly.

My stomach dropped when I pulled into her driveway and saw Emerson's truck. Could I not get away from this man? It was bad enough that he still invaded my thoughts, but I seemed to be running into him everywhere since he got back.

And I had a sneaking suspicion that Fiona was behind it.

The two of them were sitting together on her front porch. Fiona gave a little wave as I pulled up, and I thought I glimpsed guilt on her face. *Good.*

"Hey, Daphne," Emerson said as I walked up to the porch.

"Hey." I looked from him to Fiona. Yes, definite guilt.

"Isn't this a pleasant surprise?" Fiona cut in. "Emerson was nice enough to come help stack my firewood today."

I narrowed my eyes at her. I could have sworn that the man who dropped her firewood off had stayed and stacked it himself. Surely she wouldn't have undone all that work just to give Emerson a reason to be here.

Who was I kidding? This was Fiona.

"Yes," I said dryly. "Such a nice surprise. What a nice little dinner party we'll have."

"I can go," Emerson offered quietly. "I don't want to make things awkward."

I started to tell him I would go instead, but I looked at his face and something stopped me. I had seen pain on it before, but this was different altogether. The man was miserable. Raw. Hurt. And no matter what had happened between us, I didn't want him to feel that way for even one second longer. I also really didn't want him to be alone.

"No, it's okay," I said. "We can be friends, right? Besides, unless Fiona's filled you in already, I have an update on the case you might be interested in."

My words did the trick. His face changed from tortured pain to annoyance.

"The case? Seriously? I thought you said you weren't getting involved."

"I can't help it if I stumble across things accidentally. Jackson says I would make a brilliant detective." I grinned at the way his eyes darkened.

"Well, enough of that," Fiona interrupted. "It's time to pull dinner out of the oven and switch from this tea to something more appropriate. You two come on inside and wash up."

We followed obediently. I took my shoes off at the door, and Emerson followed suit. We walked to the kitchen, where Fiona handed us each a Guinness Stout, then popped one open for herself and took a long swig of it.

Emerson grinned at her with affection. "You surprise me more every time I'm around you," he said.

"Well, that's a mercy. I'd hate to ever become predictable."

"I don't think that's possible," I said. "Something smells amazing. What is it?"

"Shepherd's pie," she announced with pride. "The potatoes, carrots, peas, corn, and herbs are from my own garden, of course."

"That sounds great. Where can I wash up?" Emerson asked.

Fiona pointed him down the hallway to the bathroom.

As soon as we were alone, I cornered her. "Fiona. Moving firewood? Really?"

She sighed and shook her head. "I may have made a mess of things. The boy needed a project. Needed to help. But, I'm afraid we'll have to give up our hopes for him coming around and sweeping you off your feet again. I think it really is over. And I'm woman enough to say I'm sorry for tricking you both into dinner together. I wouldn't have done it if I'd known."

Her words stunned me. "I wasn't hoping..." I couldn't finish the lie.

She gave me a look of sympathy and squeezed my arm.

Hearing Fiona say it was over made the ache a thousand times worse than it had ever been. Fiona was the eternal optimist. Whatever her reason for saying it was over, if that's what she believed, then it really was. I trusted her judgment completely.

Emerson returned. I excused myself to wash my own hands, grateful for a minute alone. It was ridiculous. It had been weeks since he had ghosted me, and he had already told me himself that we were done. But yesterday, when he'd played knight in shining armor, I had allowed myself to hope again.

I couldn't even explain why he meant so much to me.

But my soul felt tied to his somehow. And it felt like my heart might never be whole again.

I gathered myself and joined them at the table, putting on a fake smile. Dinner was awkward at first, but Fiona did a great job of helping everyone relax. She told stories about her life and had Emerson rolling in laughter over some of her escapades. He laughed even more when I told him about the curse, and he got to witness Fiona's demonstrative eye rolls and protests.

"You know, that's interesting," he said. "I've never heard that story. But I've hiked that trail several times. I had an experience once that I've never been able to explain."

"What was it?" I asked, leaning forward with wide eyes.

"Well..." He lowered his voice and leaned forward to match me. His eyes shifted from me to Fiona and back again. "I was by myself. Had hiked up that morning. Left the clearing and found a spot in the woods where I could set up my hammock for a little afternoon siesta. The wind rocked me to sleep, and I slept like a baby. Woke up two hours later to strange sounds."

"What sounds?" My voice was a whisper.

"It was like a woman...only not exactly. Sounded like singing, or chanting, carried on the wind. Felt like it was all around me. And you know I'm not a superstitious person, but I couldn't help thinking about some of the ghost stories I had heard around the campfire as a kid."

"Wow, that's spooky." It gave me chills just thinking about it.

"Oh, the story isn't over," he said with a shake of his head. "That was only the beginning. See, I decided to try to find where the noise was coming from. Prove to myself that I was being silly, and that ghosts aren't real. So I started slowly making my way back toward the clearing. The noise got louder and more focused, like that's where it was coming from. So I quietly made my way back there and hid behind a tree to look. And do you know what I saw?"

"What?" I asked, my eyes as wide as saucers.

"There was a figure. A woman. Ghost, fairy, dryad, I don't know. But she was beautiful. One of the most beautiful visions I've ever seen, with long, flowing, white hair. She was in the clearing. Barefoot, dancing, and singing to the trees."

"Oh my word. That's unreal! You must have seen her ghost, still there haunting the clearing!" I couldn't believe it.

Fiona busted out laughing. "You little devil. I didn't know you were spying on me that day."

I looked back and forth between her and Emerson.

"Wait. You're talking about Fiona?"

He was shaking with laughter, tears in his eyes. "Yes. But you should have seen your face," he said, choking.

I shook my head, my lips pressed tight as I tried not to indulge him with a grin.

"See, Daphne, I told you there was no curse," Fiona said, poking me. "Now, I have apple pie and apple cider for dessert. Since it's such a beautiful night, how about we take it outside and have a nice little fire pit?"

"That sounds like fun," I said.

"Emerson, do you mind getting it started while I heat up the apple cider?" Fiona asked.

"No problem." He got up and grabbed his jacket, then hesitated. "Daphne, do you mind giving me a hand? I'd like to talk to you about something."

My heartbeat went just a little bit faster as hope rose again.

Chapter Nineteen

Daphne

I GRABBED MY COAT AND FOLLOWED EMERSON OUTSIDE TO Fiona's fire pit. He expertly made a little pile of kindling and stacked small pieces of wood in a pyramid shape around it. We were both quiet. The darkness felt heavy. The ease that had developed over dinner had dissipated as soon as we left the warm glow of Fiona's cottage.

He soon had a roaring fire. I moved beside it, trying to warm my heart as much as my hands.

"I owe you an explanation," he said quietly, his gaze not meeting my eyes. "I know that. And I'm sorry for not giving it to you earlier. It's painful to talk about, so I just don't. Well, until Fiona sat me down to talk today."

"She's good at that," I said with a small laugh.

"Yeah, she is," he admitted. "You know, I never really got to know her very well, despite being neighbors and all. But she's a special woman."

"She is."

He dropped his fire poker and sat heavily into one of the chairs at the pit. I took the one next to him and waited for him to speak. Any butterflies or hope were long gone—I could feel that this wasn't that kind of conversation. But I would try to be a friend, if that's what he needed.

"I told you about my brother," he began.

"Ken?" I asked.

"Yeah."

"Yes. I remember."

"There's a lot to the story I didn't tell you." He let out a little exhale. "As much as you deserve to know the whole thing, I don't have it in me to go through it all again. But the gist of it is that it's my fault he joined the Marines. And I was there when he died." He got quiet.

I placed my hand on his arm. "I can't imagine how awful that was for you."

"It was worse for him," he pointed out. "As horrible as it was to see him like that, I'm glad I was there."

I nodded and squeezed his arm.

"I made him a promise," he continued. "Since it was my fault he wasn't going to marry his sweetheart and have the life they deserved, I promised I wouldn't either. It felt like the least I could do."

I felt stunned. "But Emerson, that's—" I bit my lip before the word *ridiculous* came out.

"I don't expect you to understand," he said, his voice gruff.

"Your brother wouldn't want you to be miserable. That's not love. No matter what you think, it's not your fault he died. You know that, right? You told me not to blame myself for Don's death. But you're doing the exact same thing, and you're going to punish yourself for life because of it?"

"Like I said, I don't expect you to understand." There was an edge to his words this time. "I just wanted to explain. I moved here to get some space from all of it. Was planning on living my life, doing some good, serving my community. And all that worked out great, until you showed up and I started wanting more. But I can't have more, you see? And I'm sorry. I'm sorry I hurt you. I'm sorry for everything. It was wrong to get involved when I couldn't offer you a future, I know that. But I seem to lose my head around you," he said with a bitter laugh.

"Let me see if I understand. You're saying the only reason you ended things between us was because you think you don't deserve happiness?"

"It's because I made a promise. And I keep my promises." His voice was firm.

I just shook my head. I had no idea what to say.

He tapped his fingers on his thigh. "So, you understand now why we can't be together."

"I understand why you *think* we can't be together," I said, choosing my words carefully. "I understand that you're punishing yourself and denying yourself any future happiness because, for some reason, you think that's what your brother would want."

He didn't answer. Thankfully, Fiona emerged with a basket of provisions, saving us from the silence.

She eyed me sharply, apparently realizing she had stepped into some major tension. "Let me pour you a cup of cider, Emerson," she said brightly. "And there's whiskey in the basket if anyone wants to make theirs Irish."

"Actually, it's getting kind of late," Emerson said. "I think I'll let you two ladies enjoy the fire. I've got an early morning tomorrow." He looked at me, regret written all over his face.

Fiona spoke up. "Will you take some of that tea we talked about earlier?"

He looked her way, regret changing to affection. "I will. Thank you."

"Let me just go mix you up a little bag," she said. "I'll write directions on it so you can make it up for yourself. Try drinking one to two cups every day for a few weeks, okay? See if it helps."

He nodded. "Thanks."

She squeezed his arm and hurried back inside.

I stood, feeling the need to say something even though I didn't have the words. "Emerson, I can't say I really understand what you're going through, because I don't. I lost my dad, but losing a sibling in such a traumatic way? That's awful. I can't even imagine. But I also don't understand the promise you made. I hate to see you punishing yourself. Even if you don't want to be with me, I don't want you to be alone and unhappy your whole life. You don't deserve that."

"So you don't hate me?" There was pain behind the words—and hope, too.

"Hate you?" I let out a breath and shook my head. "No. I don't hate you. I kind of wish I did," I admitted. "That might feel a little easier."

"It's okay," he said. "I hate myself enough for the both of us."

He looked so sad, so hurt. I couldn't help myself. I moved forward and wrapped my arms around him, wishing so much that I could take some of the pain away.

He pulled me close and held me, burying his face in the crook of my neck. I closed my eyes, breathed in his scent, and let myself pretend everything was different, just for a moment.

I knew he was pretending things were different, too.

He finally broke away.

"Goodbye, Daphne," he said, looking deep into my eyes and stroking my face as if he were trying to memorize me.

"Goodbye, Emerson," I whispered.

He leaned down and kissed me softly on the forehead. I closed my eyes, unable to stop the tear that betrayed me. He brushed it away, then turned and walked to the cottage.

I watched him walk away, feeling strangely empty inside. It didn't matter how many times I reminded myself that I barely knew him, that we hadn't dated long, that it shouldn't be a big deal... It was. What I felt for him wasn't just attraction, though that was certainly there in spades.

I loved him.

And I hadn't even realized it until tonight.

But I knew he was serious when he said he kept his promises. Emerson was one of those old-fashioned, highly ethical men. I had known it since the day we'd met. He was the kind of man who kept his word, even if it meant sacrificing everything.

Oh, how I hated being that sacrifice.

I TOOK my seat at the fire and gazed at the flames, letting their flickering dance ease me into a state where I could put my thoughts away and just be. It was a beautiful, clear night, and bright stars were already appearing in the sky. I took solace in them and in the sweet smell of smoke, while I waited for Fiona.

She returned shortly and immediately pulled the whiskey from the basket. "I think we both need ours to be Irish tonight."

"Yeah, I'd say so." I sighed.

"I saw that hug," she said, pouring steaming cider into two mugs and adding a generous pour of whiskey on top. "But it didn't seem to have a happy ending."

"It was a goodbye hug." Another tear betrayed me. "He told me about his promise. It's so ridiculous, Fiona. He's told me so many times to not feel guilty about Don's death. Yet he carries the blame and punishment for his brother's?"

"Survivor's guilt is a form of PTSD, dear," she said gently. She handed me a mug and took the seat next to mine, joining me in my fire gazing. "It may not make sense to you, but it has a hold on him for sure."

"How do you know so much?" I asked. "You always seem to know everything."

"I've lived a long life," she said. She sat quietly for a moment, taking a long sip of cider before continuing. "And I've had some experience with survivor's guilt myself."

I looked over at her, curious. I only knew a snippet of Fiona's past. It was hard to imagine her as anything other than she was now.

"Do you want to talk about it?" I asked.

She shook her head. "Not tonight. We've both had heaviness aplenty for one evening."

Silence lingered as we gazed at the fire, sipping from our mugs.

"I love him," I confessed, finally breaking the quiet. "I know that's stupid."

"Now, why on earth would that be stupid?"

"Because we were together for such a short time. Because he's made it clear we don't have a future. Because he's ridiculously stubborn," I said with a little laugh.

"Well, you're kind of stubborn yourself," she teased.

"True."

"Love is never stupid," she said, her tone serious again. "And it's never wasted. It's the most powerful force on earth. I know that even if there's no happy ending for you two, your love will make a difference in his life. You may never know or see it. But it will. Because that's what love does."

"I hope so."

"It will." She reached over and patted my knee. "I know everything, remember?"

I grinned despite everything. Fiona was so good at making me feel better.

I voiced another thought, an idea that had come to me while I was sitting alone by the fire. "Fiona, I'm thinking of going home for a little while."

"Already?" She was surprised. "It's still early yet, and we just started our cider."

"Not to the house. I mean to Arkansas."

"Oh." She sounded disappointed, and I was reminded that the last time I had left Rosemary Mountain, she hadn't seen me again for twenty-one years. It had been a painful loss for her, and she had to be wondering if it was going to happen again.

"Not permanently," I said, trying to reassure her. "Just for a week or two." I quickly relayed everything Jackson had told me about potential legal trouble over the treasure.

"Oh, that Bill Brinksley is always ruining everything!" She practically spit out the words.

"So I've heard. I think I need to go look through Dad's remaining stuff. See if I can find any evidence, one way or the other. Maybe if I can go through old financial records or something... I don't know. But I feel like I need to at least try to get some answers. I'm also hoping he has more journals by Della Porter. Mom is looking for them, but she has a full-time job, and I'll be able to look faster."

I paused, taking another sip of cider. "And, well, I think getting out of here for a little while would help put some space between me and Emerson. I feel like I've been running into him everywhere since he got back, and it hurts to see him. Some time and distance would help."

"I hate to see you go, but I understand. I'll keep an eye on your place while you're gone."

"Thank you. I appreciate it. I won't be gone long."

She squeezed my hand in reply, but it hung heavy over both of us, as if we both knew that I might not come back at all.

CHAPTER TWENTY

Daphne

TWO DAYS LATER, I WAS ON THE ROAD BACK TO LITTLE Rock, a swirling mess of emotions. The break from Rosemary Mountain would do me good, at least until I could come to terms with just being Emerson's friend. I was excited to make some progress on the case. I was even looking forward to seeing Mom, which was a completely unfamiliar emotion for me. Unfamiliar, but welcome. I was grateful for the strides we had made in our relationship.

But a huge part of me was dreading even seeing Dad's house again. What was once my refuge from the world now felt like a weight hanging around my neck. And somehow, a lifetime of happy memories there had been overshadowed by memories of his illness—and the betrayal of learning about my real mother.

The trip could help me feel better about everything, or it could make everything worse. Only time would tell.

My cell phone rang, interrupting my thoughts. *Joe.*

"Hey Joe, what's up?"

"Where are you? The phone sounds funny."

"Sorry, you're on speaker. I'm driving."

"You alone?"

"Yep."

"We need to talk." His voice was flat, and I felt a wave of nerves. Had he finally found out something about my mother's death?

"I'm listening," I said, keeping my voice steady.

"I'd rather come over. When are you going to be home?"

"I'm not sure. I'm actually heading out of town."

"What? Where?" He sounded surprised.

"Back to Little Rock. I have some things I need to handle there."

He breathed a sigh of relief. "Well, that's probably a good thing. I wanted to talk to you about lying low anyway. I'm guessing you know something about this whole treasure hunt already?"

"Yeah, you could say that." I chuckled.

"It's making people crazy, Daphne. And by people, I'm talking about Bill."

I sighed. "I know, I've heard. Detective Ford warned me that Bill thinks my dad found the treasure and might come after me for it."

"I'd say he's definitely coming after you. He's raising a stink all over town, saying Lonnie stole it right out from under his nose. And while nobody likes him, he's the biggest pocketbook in this town. Has a lot of influence that way. I smell trouble coming."

"Great. Just what I need."

He hesitated for a moment. "Do you think Lonnie really might have found it?"

"Honestly? I doubt it. I don't know what he was like back when you knew him, but he's always been so proud of his historical finds. He loves to show them off. His house was practically a museum," I said, laughing. "I can't imagine him finding a treasure like that and never telling anyone that he did."

"Like a museum, huh?"

"Yeah. He was a huge collector of everything you can imagine." I smiled, thinking fondly of how excited he had always been to show me his latest find, and how fun it had been growing up surrounded by so much history and intrigue.

"Some of that stuff was probably pretty expensive, huh?"

"Well, yes," I said, not liking where he was going.

"He have some high-paying job or something?"

"He was an accountant," I said, feeling defensive.

"I know accountants make decent money, but does that add up to you?"

"Honestly, Joe, I don't know." I sighed. I felt so uncomfortable with this conversation, like I was betraying Dad.

"I'd suggest you find out," he said, his tone light. "And not just because of Bill."

"What do you mean?"

"Look, I don't want to hurt you. But look at this from my perspective. Your ma, one of the happiest people I've ever met, supposedly commits suicide for no good reason. You and I both agree that's not what happened, and you and I are both trying to find out the truth."

"What are you saying, Joe?" I didn't even try to keep the edge out of my voice this time.

"I never even considered Lonnie as a suspect. Everyone knew how hung up he was over your ma. But for many people, money trumps love. The detective in me has to think that an honest-to-goodness treasure is a pretty good motive for murder."

"He wouldn't have." My voice was firmer than my heart.

"I hope you're right. You've been through enough already without having to come to terms with something like that. But while you're in Little Rock, why don't you see what you can find out about his finances? Hopefully, you can rule the whole thing out. But, Daphne, we both agreed we would not stop looking until we found out who killed Eileen. And if the reason we've gotten nowhere is that we've been looking in the wrong place..."

I couldn't answer. Not right away. He waited. Like Fiona, he was good at that, although I knew it came from a different place. Fiona's patience was from compassion. Joe was a skilled interrogator who knew that people would talk to him. Eventually.

"Look, I don't believe there's any chance that my dad killed Eileen," I said firmly. "But I was already planning on looking into his finances because of the Bill thing. I need to know what I might be facing. So yeah, I'll dig. And I'm planning on digging into the treasure thing from another angle, too."

"Oh, yeah?" His voice was mild. "What angle would that be?"

"I got to talk to Julie, the girlfriend of the guy who was killed. She said he told his research partner about the treasure. I did a little searching online and found out who the partner was. He has office hours at the university today. I left practically in the middle of the night so that I can get there and talk to him."

Joe chuckled. "Man, you remind me of your ma. Just like her, you know. She would have done the same thing."

I smiled. "Anyway, I'm hoping to find out more about what the journal said and where the treasure might be located. Or anything he knows, really. The more I know, the more chance I have of figuring out if Dad really did have it."

"Good work. Let me know what you find. And be careful."

"I don't think you have anything to worry about," I said, laughing. "For once, I'll actually be far, far away from the killer."

It was late afternoon when I parked my car at the university where Wesley and his research partner worked. I was thrilled that guest parking was a decent walk from the history building. It gave me a chance to stretch my legs after the long car ride, and to experience that feeling that only seems to exist on college campuses. This particular campus was gorgeous, with old brick buildings and dappled sunlight shining through the branches of stately, mature trees. Students milled around on the lawn, reading, chatting, or playing frisbee. Couples held hands and strolled the sidewalks, soaking up time together.

I loved college. It was the last time in my life that things had been simple.

I found the history building and made my way up the stairs to the third floor where Steve Wallace, Wesley's partner, had his office. Class let out, and the stairwell was flooded with students laughing, talking, and rushing to their next class. I smiled watching them.

Steve's office door was cracked open. I knocked and he told me to come in without even looking up. He was standing behind his desk, stuffing papers into his briefcase.

And he was movie-star gorgeous.

"Mr. Wallace?"

"Yes?" he answered abruptly, before looking up. When he did, a slow grin spread across his face. "Well, hello there," he said, in a different tone altogether. "I don't believe you're one of my students. I would have remembered you."

"Oh, no," I said with a small laugh. "I'm not a student here at all. I was actually wondering if I could ask you some questions about a historical artifact that my dad owned." I offered him an innocent-looking smile, letting my eyes go wide. "I've been told you're the person to ask."

"Well, you've come to the right place," he said, still flashing that grin. He was gorgeous, yes—and it was clear he knew it. "Unfortunately, I'm late for a meeting."

"Oh, I'm sorry. I thought these were your office hours."

"Normally, they are. But I've been out of town. Playing hooky, I guess you could say." He winked at me, as if he were the most clever person on earth. "I missed a faculty meeting last week, and I'm afraid I have to make up for it now."

"Oh," I said, trying to mask my surprise. My mind was racing. Was it possible he'd been in Rosemary Mountain? He could be a legitimate suspect. "I love traveling. Where did you go? Did you have a nice vacation?" It sounded lame, even to me.

"Working trip. And as I said, I'm running late." His words were pointed, dismissing me.

I had to try one more time. "I'm so sorry, I know you have important things to do." I was practically cooing. "Is there a convenient time for me to come back? I would just love to talk to you." I gave him a bashful smile, looking up at him through fluttering eyelashes. It was absolutely ridiculous. But I could tell by his grin that he was loving every minute of it.

"Tell you what. Meet me back here tomorrow night. Say, around seven? We'll go to dinner, and you can ask me all your questions." He grinned again, as if offering me the world.

"Oh, that sounds wonderful." I kept up the cooing. "I can't wait."

He ushered me out and locked the door behind me.

· · ·

I LEFT campus and drove to Dad's house—my house, I reminded myself. It was still so strange that he wouldn't be there.

From the outside, it looked the same. The lawn maintenance service was doing a good job. It looked just as friendly and warm as ever, like Dad could step out on the porch and wave to me again. It felt surreal.

But inside was a different story. Between what I had taken to the cottage and what had already sold or been donated, more than half of his furnishings and possessions were gone. Sales tags hung from the items that remained. It felt cold, empty, and sad.

I dropped my bags and called Mom to let her know I had arrived.

"Oh, good!" she said. "You made great time."

"Yeah, I left early and drove fast." I looked around the sad dining room. "Hey, do you want to go out for dinner tonight? I know we planned on you bringing takeout, but, well, the house feels kind of depressing. Maybe we could go somewhere instead, before we dive into searching."

"Sure, that's fine." She hesitated for just a moment. "Daphne, do you maybe want to come stay with me instead of staying there? You know I have a guest room..."

The offer caught me off guard. As odd as it sounded, I had never stayed over at her house. Since she wasn't my legal parent, Dad had retained sole custody after their divorce. Unaware of the truth, I grew up assuming she simply didn't want me. And even now, the idea of staying with her had never even crossed my mind.

But with a glance at the house, already staged for the next estate sale, I decided it might not be a terrible idea.

"Actually," I said, "I would really love that. Thank you for offering."

"Of course! It will be fun." She sounded both pleased and relieved that her offer was accepted. Another sign of just how far we had come since Dad's death. "Tell you what, meet me at Cantina Laredo a few minutes after five. I'll head straight there after work."

"Sounds perfect. See you then."

A GLANCE at my watch confirmed that I had a good hour before I needed to leave. That was plenty of time to get in some searching. I started with the bookshelves that remained in Dad's study. I had taken as many of them as I could fit into the cottage, but three cases remained. I looked carefully over every title. There were plenty of antiques, and even a couple of other old journals. But nothing by Della Porter and nothing that seemed to be related to the treasure, as far as I could tell. I hoped Steve could give me more information about who this famous robber was. The cell phone pictures I had snapped of the journal didn't give me much to go on, so it was hard to know what I was looking for.

I headed to the attic next. The attic was where I had found the box with pictures of my mother. Knowing that, it made sense that if Dad had a treasure or something that pointed to it, he would have kept it up there in the one place I wasn't free to go as a child. I had given everything a once-over already when I was choosing what to keep and what to sell. But again, not knowing what I was looking for, it was very possible I could have missed something important.

I only hoped that if something crucial was there, the estate company hadn't already found and sold it.

Or kept it.

At first glance, the attic seemed as dusty and untouched as ever, a good sign. But none of my searching revealed anything that seemed to be connected to Della or the gold.

My cell phone alarm rang, letting me know I had to wrap up and get ready for dinner.

I closed the door to the attic and headed back downstairs, grateful to be away from its ghosts.

MOM WAS ALREADY SEATED when I arrived at the restaurant. She jumped up to give me a hug—another surprise, considering how little affection we had shown each other when I was growing up. I hugged her back, pleased by how happy I was to see her.

"You look great," I said. It was true. She seemed younger, fresher.

"Thanks. You look better than the last time I saw you, too." She smiled, her cheeks pink. "Physically, anyway. But you seem sad. Want to talk about it?"

I took a sip of the margarita she had already ordered me. I didn't actually like margaritas, but I knew she had no way of knowing that.

"Things have kind of taken a turn," I said, swirling my glass.

"What kind of turn? Are you talking about you and Emerson?"

"No, I wasn't, although things kind of took a turn there as well. That's definitely over," I said, sighing. "But I don't want to talk about that right now."

"What's going on?" She leaned forward, concern in her eyes.

I quickly recapped the issues with Bill Brinksley and shared Joe's concerns with her.

"I don't know," I said, massaging my temples as if it could somehow ease the real tension within me. "I can't imagine Dad being involved in Eileen's death. Can you?"

She took entirely too long to answer.

"Mom?"

"Of course not," she said finally. "I don't think your father was a killer. And I believe he truly loved your mother. But I also think your father was more complicated than you ever realized."

"Complicated how?"

"He could be cruel," she said quietly.

"Wait, did he hurt you?" My voice rose in anger and shock.

"No, no." She waved me down, glancing around nervously. Janet couldn't stand a scene. "Not physically anyway. But, well, you know our marriage wasn't happy. It doesn't matter. All that's a long way from murder."

I knew there was more there, but I didn't want to cause her any embarrassment by pushing. So I left it and took a different angle. "Talk to me about the money situation when you guys got married. I was way too little to remember any of it. Was he rich?"

"I wouldn't say rich, necessarily," she said, choosing her words carefully. "But financially independent, yes. At least it seemed that way. Honestly, Daphne, he kept me in the dark about our finances. In the beginning, that was one of the things I found so attractive about him. It swept me off my feet. I was only nineteen, you see, and having someone who seemed so secure promise to take care of me was very appealing. He took me to nice restaurants, and was always dressed well.

He paid for everything, of course. And when we got married, he managed all the bills and accounts. He gave me an allowance for household and personal spending. I had nothing to do with the money beyond that."

"Hmm." My brows furrowed as I thought it over. "Was he an accountant already? There's not a college in Rosemary Mountain, so I assumed he went to school after he moved away."

"No, he wasn't," she said. "He went to school shortly after we got married, since he had a built-in babysitter."

I bit my lip at the bitterness in her voice. She immediately caught it and reached out a hand.

"Daphne, my anger isn't about you. I meant it when I said that you were the only good thing that marriage ever gave me. I just hate that I let him trick me into thinking he was madly in love when the truth is that he could barely stand being in the same room as me. If he had actually loved me, I would have been the happiest woman in the world staying home, taking care of you. But a lifetime of rejection is a hard burden to bear."

"I know," I said quietly, taking another sip of the awful margarita.

Mom realized my meaning and looked at me with eyes full of regret.

"It's fine. Let's just move on from that." I didn't want to cause her more pain, and I didn't much feel like stewing in my own either. "So he went back to school after you got married. How did he pay for school? Where did his money come from? Do you have any idea?"

She shrugged. "I assumed a small trust fund or family money of some sort. But don't misunderstand. We were always comfortable, but not millions-in-buried-gold comfortable. There was enough that he paid cash for my car, but I know he took out a mortgage for the house."

"That might not mean anything," I pointed out. "If he knew the money wasn't really his, he could have been only spending small amounts so as not to draw attention or raise questions."

"That's true," she admitted. She leaned forward, glancing around to make sure no one was paying attention to us. "What does the sight tell you?"

It caught me off guard. Dad had told me to kill the sight when I was a kid. And though I had told Mom about it when it returned, I knew she wasn't entirely comfortable with the idea. It wasn't something I was used to talking about with her.

"Nothing at all, so far. I've only had one vision in the last few weeks, and it was of the victim fighting with his girlfriend. It helped me find her. But no information about Dad, Eileen, or anything. Honestly, I'm getting really frustrated and wondering why I even moved out there."

She looked at me with empathy and placed her hand over mine. "You moved out there to find the truth. And look how far you've come!"

"It doesn't feel like I've made any progress at all."

"That's not true," she insisted. "You may not have found your mother's killer yet, but you have confirmation that she was, in fact, killed. That's something. And you have help now, looking into it."

"Yes," I admitted begrudgingly. "Don't get me wrong. I'm grateful for all of that. But sometimes I wonder how things would have played out if I had just put that box back into the attic and pretended I never found it. If I had decided to stay in Dad's house and make it my own. I don't know. I'm kind of thinking about just moving back here and starting over." The words came out before I meant them to, but I realized as I said them that they were true.

She cocked her head. "You've never wanted to live in that big old house by yourself. You were so sure when you bought the cottage. What's changed?"

"Everything?" My eyes filled with tears. "Mom, I've lost half of my clients."

Her face went blank. "What?"

"Apparently, my work was less than stellar when I was being drugged," I said with a bitter laugh.

"But that's not your fault. Did you explain?"

"Sure. But you have to admit, if one of your contractors told you that their work performance tanked because they were unknowingly being drugged against their will, would you automatically believe them and trust that everything was going to get better?"

"No," she admitted. "I would assume they had a problem with drugs, refused to take personal responsibility, and had a high likelihood of relapse."

"Exactly." I picked at a loose thread on the tablecloth. "Anyway, between that and Dad's house not selling, things are a bit, um, strained at the moment. And now Emerson is back in town, and I keep running into him everywhere..." My eyes filled with tears again. "I don't know, Mom. Yes, I've found some answers, but it seems like everything in my life has fallen apart since I moved there."

"Not everything," she said gently, squeezing my hand again. "I don't think you and I would have gotten as far as we have if you hadn't moved there. Everything that happened forced us to talk, *really* talk, for the first time, didn't it?"

"You're probably right about that," I admitted.

"And you seem so happy there. You fit. You blossomed into someone more confident, more sure of herself, more willing to try new things."

"I don't feel very confident right now." My voice cracked.

"I know." She nodded sadly.

"I haven't decided anything for sure," I said. "But I think the cottage might sell more quickly than the house here. More and more people are looking for land, and it's in way better shape now than when I bought it. Houses with acreage in Rosemary Mountain are still selling quickly. It would be a huge cash infusion that could take the pressure off and give me time to reestablish here."

"If it's all about money, let me give you some," she suggested.

"Thanks, but no," I said firmly. "Whatever I decide, I need to, well, stand on my own two feet, you know?"

"I know," she said with a smile playing on her lips. "That's one reason I know Rosemary Mountain has been good for you."

"It's been a growth experience for sure," I agreed.

She changed the subject after that, to my relief, chattering about an upcoming gala she was helping plan. I tried to attend to the conversation, but worry filled the back of my mind.

Our conversation had done nothing to relieve my fears about what Joe had suggested.

If anything, I doubted my dad more than ever.

Chapter Twenty-One

Daphne

The next night, I told Mom I was having dinner with a friend. I felt guilty for not telling her the whole story. Normally, I would have told her what I was up to, but since Steve had admitted to being out of town when Wes was killed, she would have freaked out.

I was a little freaked out, too, to be honest.

But I needed information. I had spent the whole day searching Dad's house and still hadn't found anything that seemed even remotely related to Della Porter or the treasure hunt. So I promised myself I would stay on guard and be careful, but I had to question Steve.

Just to be on the safe side, I decided to make Greg aware of my plans. My first thought was to tell Jackson instead—he seemed to actually encourage my investigative tendencies, and would be less likely to criticize me for my idea. But I feared that if he knew what I was up to and something went wrong, he would take the fall for it. Better to go over Jackson's head and give him deniable plausibility.

Or something like that.

So I sent a quick text to Greg:

Hey Greg. It's Daphne. I'm in Little Rock visiting Mom. I'm having dinner tonight with Wesley Adams' old research partner, Steve Wallace. Thought I would ask him about the treasure hunt, see if I could find out anything. I'll let you know if I do. FYI, he's been out of town... just got back... I'll try to find out where he was. Okay! See you later!

I sent the text, then turned my phone to silent so that I could ignore any reply. Plausible deniability for me, too.

Steve's building was eerily quiet and empty when I climbed the steps to meet him at seven. I was so used to the hustle and bustle of class hours on campus that it was unnerving how quiet it was. The classrooms were all dark, and half the hall lights were off. I had to fight off my growing nerves just to make it to his office.

His door was cracked. I knocked timidly and poked my head in.

He looked up, momentarily confused, before the light dawned on his face. "Ahhh, yes! My lovely dinner date. I had completely forgotten." He shot me that practiced movie-star smile, the one he seemed confident would knock me off my feet.

"Well, that sure doesn't make a girl feel very good," I said, matching his flirtatious tone.

"Oh, you know us professor types. We're always a bit scattered, I'm afraid." He gestured around his office with false self-deprecation. "But I assure you, I'll make it up to you." There was that smile again. I wondered how many women had fallen for that charm.

He grabbed his jacket and pulled it on, then came to me at the doorway.

"You know, I just realized I don't even know your name," he said. His voice was actually hesitant, and his smile seemed more genuine this time, as if the confident mask he wore had slipped momentarily. I hoped he would keep it off.

"Daphne," I said. "Daphne Sullivan."

I watched for any trace of recognition at the name, not knowing what exactly Wesley had shared with him. But his eyes didn't betray any flicker of knowledge.

"Steve Wallace," he said, shaking my hand quickly. There was a brief, genuine grin before that movie star smile came back. "Shall we go?"

He gestured for me to lead the way with one hand, while the other went to the small of my back, gently guiding me.

It made me think of Emerson, who used to do the same.

"Where did you park?" he asked.

"Out front, by the fountain."

"I'm behind this building. Faculty parking. We can take my car, and I'll bring you back to yours after dinner."

I was instantly uncomfortable with the suggestion. I didn't know this man at all, and to my mind at least, he was a suspect in Wesley's murder.

"Oh no," I protested. "I don't want to take up too much of your time. I'll meet you wherever we're going, and then you won't have to go to so much trouble."

"Nonsense, it's no trouble at all," he said, flashing that pretty smile at me. "I insist. My mother taught me to be a gentleman, after all."

A true gentleman would recognize my discomfort.

I quickly calculated the risks. Greg knew who I was with—but Steve didn't know that, so that wouldn't give me any protection. There had to be security cameras on campus, though, that would see me leaving with him. Surely someone smart enough to be a professor wouldn't be dumb enough to kill someone he had just been recorded with. Right?

With a small sigh of annoyance, I agreed and let him lead me to his car.

AN HOUR LATER, I was on my second glass of wine and still hadn't had a chance to ask Steve anything at all. He had been much too busy telling me his life story.

He was charming, that was certain. I felt sure he was used to women eating every bit of this up. Women, or maybe college girls who idolized him for his looks.

Meanwhile, I had a massive headache brewing and was afraid I might need a third glass to get through the evening.

When he finally paused for breath, I interrupted him, the wine making me bold. "Well, Mr. Wallace—"

"Steve, please," he said. "Only my students call me Mr. Wallace. Unless, you know, you're into that kind of thing, in which case, you're welcome to keep it up." He wiggled his eyebrows and winked at me. I fought back a grimace.

"Steve." I forced a smile. "I wanted to talk to you about a historical item that my father owned."

"Oh yes. I had almost forgotten that was why you came knocking on my office door to begin with." Another wink.

"Right. Anyway..." I took a deep breath and decided to just lay it all out on the table. "Your research partner, Wesley Adams, bought a diary from my father's estate."

A quick look flickered across his face—regret? Sadness? I wasn't sure. It was quickly replaced with his practiced smile. "Oh, is this what that's about? You're a treasure seeker!"

"Not exactly, but I'm trying to learn as much as possible."

He gave me an amused grin. "Right. So what do you want to know?"

"Well..." I lifted my hands helplessly. "I guess everything. I know the journal belonged to a woman named Della Porter and that he thought it held the clues to buried treasure. I know he was in Rosemary Mountain looking for it. I've seen the journal, but haven't gotten a chance to read it for myself. What can you tell me about it?"

"Well, first off, I think this whole idea about buried treasure was nonsense. From what I know about Logan, I don't think he was the type to save up any significant amount of money. Spent it as quickly as he, ahem, *earned* it."

"Logan? Who's Logan?"

He stared at me for a second. "Wow, you really don't know anything, do you? Harvey Logan."

My face remained blank.

"Harvey Logan?" he repeated. "Also known as Kid Curry?"

I simply shrugged. I had no idea what he was talking about.

"Tiger of the Wild Bunch Gang? Rode with Butch Cassidy and the Sundance Kid?"

"Those last two sound familiar. Cowboys, right?"

"Outlaws," he corrected. "The Wild Bunch was the most successful gang of train robbers that ever existed."

"I see," I said, putting the pieces together. "Ju—someone mentioned to me that Wes thought the journal writer was in a relationship with a robber."

"I know all about Julie. You don't have to protect Wesley's secret from me." He rolled his eyes.

I offered him a small smile.

"Anyway," he continued, "Wes read that journal and decided that the name Della Porter was a pseudonym. He thought the journal was written by Logan's girlfriend, Annie Rogers. AKA Della Moore. AKA Maude Williams." He chuckled.

"I'm guessing by your tone that you disagree?"

He gave a little sigh and tilted his head back and forth like he wasn't sure. "It's a good theory," he admitted. "Annie had obviously used the name Della before, and Porter was the last name of her madame in Texas. And if it's true, it will be an amazing find. But the thing is, it's easy to make up theories about history. Change one little thing, make one little supposition, and you can come up with theories that completely rewrite what we think we know. But most of the time, it's all just our own imagination coming up with things."

The mask had completely slipped away. Instead of the arrogant professor who thought he was God's gift to women, the man sitting in front of me actually seemed human. I liked him significantly better this way.

"So you're saying it's possible, but not proven?"

"Exactly," he said. "Wes was so excited about this theory. If it's true, it's the kind of thing that Hollywood will make movies about. But I tend to look at things with a more skeptical view."

"Okay. So, since I'm sadly uninformed about these people, can you give me a quick rundown?"

"Sure. As I said, Harvey Logan was the wildest, craziest member of the Wild Bunch—the most violent by far. Murdered multiple people. Also had a reputation for enjoying prostitutes."

"Oh, so there's a connection right away," I said, leaning forward. I was starting to enjoy this conversation. "I spoke with our town librarian, who said Della Porter worked at a brothel in Rosemary Mountain."

Steve cocked his head. "I didn't know that one, but that is an interesting coincidence, isn't it? Anyway, lore has it that while Logan was a successful train robber, he never kept his money long. Spent it all in brothels. In fact, he spent so much time and money on women that multiple prostitutes named him as the father of their children. There were supposedly eighty-five 'Curry Kids,' as they called them."

"Eighty-five kids?" My jaw dropped. "Wow, he really did like the women."

Steve laughed. "Yeah. I think only five of them were proven to really be his, but who knows? Anyway, he met Annie Rogers. She started working at brothels here in Arkansas, actually."

"Arkansas? Really?"

"Yep. Mena, Arkansas, at the age of fifteen."

"Wow, that's so sad." I thought about my own life in Arkansas at fifteen. I couldn't imagine being forced into such a thing at that age.

"Yeah. Things were different for women back then. But then she met Harvey Logan. He was going by Kid Curry at that point, which is how most people know him. They hit it off, and she left prostitution and traveled with him."

"So they found love," I said softly.

"Maybe," he agreed. "Maybe love, maybe just a business arrangement. Hard to say. Things get a little hazy after that. We know they both ended up in Tennessee because they were both arrested there. But there's no proof they were still together at that point or that they even saw each other."

"What were they arrested for?" I was now fully invested in this story.

"The law had been after Logan for years. In 1901, we know he was in Knoxville, going by the name William Wilson. He was courting Laura Cross, a respectable woman. Told her he made his money in the railroad business."

I couldn't help but grin. "I mean, I guess that wasn't a total lie."

Steve grinned back. "No, it wasn't. Logan said he wanted to get married and become a farmer. Maybe he was tired of the old life, or maybe it was all just a cover for something he was planning. Maybe he had moved on from Annie Rogers, or maybe she didn't expect him to be faithful, considering her occupation. I don't know. But that December, the police got called to a brawl. Logan was there. He escaped, but got caught two days later in Jefferson City. Now, this is where the story gets good."

I leaned forward, ready to hear more.

"He was such a phenomenon that thousands wanted to visit him in jail. The sheriff allowed open visitation until the day of his trial. On December twentieth, they counted over one thousand visitors that day alone."

My jaw dropped. "Wow! So he was a celebrity?"

"Something like that." Steve laughed. "Everyone wanted to get a look at the tiger of the Wild Bunch. At his trial, he was sentenced to twenty years of hard labor and was going to be moved to the federal pen in Columbus."

"So he went away for twenty years? Did he die in prison?"

"Nope." Steve's eyes twinkled. "Never even went. There are two stories about how he got out of jail. One story says he bribed a jail guard with eight thousand dollars. My personal favorite is that he lassoed the jail guard around the neck with a wire strip taken from a broom, then let himself out of the cell and made the jailer saddle the sheriff's horse for him. Rode right through town on it before getting away."

My jaw dropped again. "Wow. That takes some balls."

"Yes, it does." He chuckled. "The truth is probably a combination of the two stories. Either way. Hell of a story."

"You said Annie was arrested, too. What happened there?"

He grinned again, obviously enjoying the story as much as I was. I greatly preferred this version of him. It was a shame his normal persona was so arrogant and self-absorbed.

"Annie got arrested in Nashville for passing banknotes associated with one of Logan's robberies. Gave the sheriff a made-up story about some other man—kept them going on it long enough for Logan to get away. Thought she had them all fooled. You have to picture her. She was twenty-six at the time, described as thin with a head full of dark brown hair, high cheekbones, and fiery eyes. She even had two gold teeth. Quite a character, if you can imagine. She flirted with everyone in the courtroom until the day she realized they knew the truth."

I grinned, picturing it. "She sounds fun."

"Apparently. Her trial was dramatic. They showed a picture of Logan, which was officially identified as him by multiple witnesses in the trial. In the photograph, there was a hand resting on his shoulder. The lawyer eventually whipped out the other half of the photo, revealing that Annie Rogers herself was the one in the photo with him."

I shook my head, eyes wide. "Sounds better than TV!"

"History usually is." His smile was so real. It was obvious he loved his vocation. "But despite all that, she was acquitted of any actual crime. She admitted to their affair. Said he gave her over five hundred dollars and bought her lots of fancy clothes. Logan sent in a written deposition backing up her story. The defense painted her as a woman who was unknowingly taken in by a clever criminal."

"Based on what you've told me about her, I don't believe that for a minute," I said.

"Me either." He grinned again. "I think they were a hell of a team."

"So, she was acquitted, and he escaped. Did they get back together after that?" I knew we were talking about an outlaw and a prostitute—the "bad guys" of the story. Even so, I found myself rooting for them.

He shrugged. "The official version is that Logan committed suicide in 1904 to avoid being recaptured. But there are other stories. One version has him going to South America with Butch Cassidy and the Sundance Kid. Another wild theory has him and Annie meeting up again, getting married, and having eight kids. But there's no proof at all of that. Most historians think Annie returned to Arkansas and went back into prostitution after being acquitted, then eventually moved to Texas. The belief is that she changed her name and went back to working for Fannie Porter. We know she wrote to Logan while he was in jail, but there's no evidence they ever saw each other again. No one really knows for sure what happened to her after that. It's hard to say with someone who keeps changing her name."

"Hmm..." I mulled things over. "But Wesley believed the journal was written by her?"

"Yeah. He believed she had all of Logan's remaining gold and that she had hidden it on Rosemary Mountain. I think he even hoped the crazy theories of Logan faking his death and marrying her were true."

"Well, you're right," I said, with a shake of my head. "If that's true, Hollywood will end up making a movie about it."

He nodded, looking annoyed. "Yeah."

"I wish I could have read the journal. Just knowing the story makes me want to read it."

"It probably wasn't the real Annie Rogers," he said gently. "But, I must confess, I would like to read it too."

"You mean you haven't?" I was surprised. He knew so much about the whole thing, I assumed Wesley had shared it with him.

"Sadly, no. Wes wouldn't let me." There was a trace of bitterness in his voice. "He didn't want to share any credit for finding it."

"I see," I said softly. I had gotten so caught up in the story that I had completely forgotten I was sitting here with a potential murderer—one with an excellent motive.

"I guess a find like that would make a career?" I asked, prodding.

"Oh yes. It would be a tremendous boon. In this day and age, it could launch the kind of career few historians can even dream of. Television, social media followers, glory, and opportunity for adventure around the world." His lips were tight. It was clear he was jealous.

"Well, I guess that didn't work out, did it?" I commented, keeping my tone casual.

"No," he said. "If it turns out that Wesley's wild idea was actually true, then either the truth will stay buried forever, or someone else will get the fame and glory."

His face twisted into an ugly smile, and a shiver of fear ran through me.

Chapter Twenty-Two

Emerson

Greg was already nursing a pint of Guinness when I got to O'Malley's. I signaled to the waitress to bring me one and slid into the booth across from him.

"You're late," Greg complained.

I glanced at my watch. "Dude. Fifteen minutes."

"Late is late."

I rolled my eyes. "Sorry. I forgot you're an old man now. Did I make you miss the senior citizen special?"

Greg flipped me off and grinned. "You're in a good mood," he commented.

"Yeah." I smiled. For the first time in a while, it felt easy.

"I don't guess it's a certain woman who's putting that smile on your face?" He smirked, then lifted his beer in salute.

I grinned. "Yes, as a matter of fact. But not the woman you're thinking of."

Fiona got all the credit as far as I was concerned, but I wasn't about to admit to him I was drinking one of her miracle teas—or that it was actually working. The grief was easing somehow. I didn't really believe it was because of a plant. Probably some sort of placebo effect. She told me it would help, and my mind wanted to believe it, so it was creating feelings of relief. But placebo or not, I was feeling better, and I was grateful to Fiona for that.

Greg's eyes narrowed. "You haven't met someone else, have you? I didn't think you were the kind of guy to move on so quickly."

"Of course not. It's not like that." I waved him off. "Look, can we talk about something other than my improved mood?"

"Sure." He grinned again.

The waitress placed my beer in front of me, and I took an appreciative sip as Greg's phone buzzed. He picked it up to read the incoming text, then groaned.

"What is it?" I asked.

He slid the phone across the table for me to read.

"Your girlfriend—sorry, *ex*-girlfriend—is going to be the death of me," he muttered under his breath.

I read the message from Daphne, and my good mood vanished. "So you're just letting her have dinner with potential murder suspects now, to see if they have an alibi? Why not swear her in as a deputy? Give her a gun. I'm sure that won't end badly." My voice came out in a growl. "Who cares that she hasn't had any training whatsoever? She's a full-blown detective now, right?" I drained half the beer, then set the mug down on the table with more force than strictly necessary.

"I'm not 'letting' her do anything, Emerson. This is the first I'm hearing about any of this. What do you expect me to do? Stop a private citizen from having dinner with another private citizen in another state, *five hundred miles away*?"

Yes.

He started typing on his phone, a frown on his face.

"What are you telling her?"

"To stay home and leave the investigation to us," he muttered. "And I'm contacting Detective Ford to see if he knows anything about this Steve Wallace."

I told myself to stay out of it. But I immediately ignored that and picked up my own phone. Maybe she would answer if I called.

Idiot. You're the last person whose call she'll take. You gave up that right, remember?

I tried anyway.

"She's not answering," I told Greg. A stab of panic hit my chest. Daphne was potentially placing herself in danger, and there wasn't anything I could do about it.

I felt helpless.

And I hated it.

"You know how she is," he said mildly. "Probably put her phone on silent right after she hit send on that text. Once she gets an idea into her head, there's no stopping her. I'm sure she's fine, Emerson."

I nodded, my lips tight. He was right, of course. The higher part of my brain knew that. But the rest of my brain was firing off all the fight-or-flight signals, which was a terrible feeling when the enemy was out of my reach.

"Jackson's just around the corner," he said. "He'll be here in a minute. We'll see if he has any info about this Wallace guy."

I SPENT the next few minutes brooding over what was left of my beer, in no mood to talk as we waited for Jackson to arrive. The silence was awkward, and Greg was clearly relieved when Jackson finally showed.

I wasn't.

Jackson greeted us both, then pulled a chair up to our booth while Greg gave him a rundown of the text he got from Daphne.

When Greg finished, Jackson's face broke into a wide grin. "Man, she's quite a woman, isn't she? She's got good instincts, and she just gets right in there."

I wanted to punch him in the face. Knock that grin right off of him. "Quite a woman? She's out to dinner with a potential murderer." My voice was all growl again. I couldn't even control it.

"I don't think so," Jackson said. "I've already looked into the partner angle." He pulled out his cell phone and started looking through it for something. "I don't have final confirmation on his alibi, but either it holds up, or he went to a whole lot of trouble to fake it."

He handed me his phone with a social media app pulled up. It was the feed of a man who was obviously into himself. Expensive haircut, perfect smile. Selfies posted almost every single day. And all the recent ones were of him in the Bahamas. Sandy beaches, mojitos, and him in a variety of swimsuits, hats, sunglasses, and vacation wear. It was like a beach vacation advertisement, except that every single picture featured him.

"The guy's profile is public," Jackson explained. "Looks like he's trying to become an influencer or something. Unless he faked all those photos, his alibi will hold. I'm verifying it, of course," he said, with a glance toward Greg. "But I don't think he's our guy."

Some of the tightness in my chest eased.

Some.

He might not be a murderer, but I still hated the thought of him taking Daphne out for dinner.

And I still wanted to punch Jackson in the face.

AFTER DINNER, I drove back to my cabin, dropped everything, and went inside to change clothes for a run. My good mood was gone. I had called Daphne three times—embarrassing enough, but made worse by the fact that she hadn't called me back, not that I blamed her. Plus, Jackson had stayed to eat with me and Greg, which had successfully ruined my night.

I couldn't forget how his face broke into a grin when he found out Daphne was investigating. He wouldn't have had that reaction if he had watched her almost die. If he had been the one helpless on the floor, witnessing the whole thing but unable to do a damn thing to save her.

Helpless.

It was the feeling I hated most in this world.

When I sat down to lace up my running shoes, Thor came up and buried his head in my lap. I stopped, cracking a little smile at his hopeful look. I scratched him behind the ears and under the chin, feeling a little better already. It was impossible to stay angry with him around.

"Not this time, bud," I said. His face drooped, making me feel guilty. But at eight years old, his hips weren't what they used to be, and it was short walks only for him from here on out.

I gave him a few more scratches and belly rubs before heading out for my run. Even though I knew she wasn't there—or maybe *because* I knew she wasn't there—I turned to the right at the end of the driveway, heading up the mountain toward Daphne's cottage.

I wanted to go there, though, for the life of me, I didn't know why. Being there would hurt like hell. Even so, I was tempted to go sit on her porch, pretend she was there, and that everything was how it should be.

Should be. The thought stabbed me in the heart.

If I had known I was going to meet her, I never would have made that promise to my brother. And maybe it was because of Fiona's tea, or maybe I was just finally dealing with the grief, but I was starting to realize what a stupid promise it really was. Forcing myself to be alone wouldn't bring my brother back, and it wouldn't repay Sarah for his death. It accomplished nothing except keeping me miserable.

Truth was, I think that's what I'd wanted in the beginning. It's what I believed I deserved.

But something inside me was shifting. A little seed of hope had been planted. If I were really honest, I would admit that seed was born the day I met Daphne and felt a connection to her that I couldn't explain. I thought I'd successfully killed that hope when I went back to Wisconsin and submerged myself in guilt all over again.

But it wasn't dead. I could feel it coming back to life, this bit of hope that maybe I could be happy. That maybe my brother wouldn't want me to sacrifice everything in his honor. Maybe it was okay to let go of this guilt and anger and actually be the person I wanted to be.

Maybe I could finally forgive myself and have a future after all...and maybe, just maybe, there was still a chance of that future including a certain woman I couldn't seem to stop thinking about—if I hadn't already screwed things up for good.

I changed my course and headed down Fiona's driveway. If anyone knew how to help me work through these thoughts, it would be her. Somehow, I knew she would have the right thing to say, the right words to put it into perspective. She probably even had an herb on her shelf just for forgiveness and letting go.

I jogged up her front steps and knocked on her door. The lights were on, and her truck was in the driveway, but there was no answer.

I knocked again and called her name.

Still nothing. No noises or movement inside.

Something felt wrong. I knocked harder and called louder, as worry rose.

Helpless.

I tried the door—locked.

I jogged around to the back, confirming my fears. Her back door was wide open, the storm door swinging in the wind. There was no sign of her in the yard.

I ran inside, calling for her.

But she was gone.

Chapter Twenty-Three

Daphne

By the time Steve brought me back to my car, I was enjoying the night much more than I had expected. He was actually an interesting guy to talk to once he dropped the whole heart-throb professor act and was just, well, himself. I didn't know why he felt the need to put on such a show all the time. The real him was way better than the persona he had adopted.

And while I couldn't be certain—after all, I had been fooled before—I really didn't think he had anything to do with Wesley's murder. He had motive, for sure. In fact, it surprised me he hadn't swooped in and taken over the treasure hunt. Getting the public credit and launching his own career seemed exactly like something his movie-star persona would eat up. But he hadn't rushed in to get the scoop. I didn't know whether to take him at his word that he simply didn't believe Wesley's theory, or if there was more to the story than he was telling me. Either way, my gut said he was innocent—of murder at least.

Even so, when he tried to kiss me goodnight, I turned my head, put a hand on his chest, and gently pushed him away. "I'm sorry," I said. "Dinner was great, and I really enjoyed talking to you. But..."

"But what?" He looked shocked. He obviously wasn't used to being shot down.

"I'm just not looking for anything more than conversation right now."

"It's just a kiss. It's no big deal."

I gave him a half smile. "I guess it is to me." My mind instantly went to Emerson and the way he had kissed me before leaving for Wisconsin. Our last kiss. If I had known it was the last, I don't think I could have let him go.

No, casual kissing wasn't for me.

"Well, okay then," Steve said. He pulled away, hurt.

I opened my car door, then turned around to him. "Can I give you some advice?"

"Sure, I guess."

"Drop the act. You're actually a nice guy when you aren't pretending to be God's gift to women. If you would stop trying to play this character you've created, you might find something real. And then, kissing might actually mean something to you."

He looked taken aback. "Maybe I'm not looking for anything real."

I shrugged. "That's a shame. You don't know what you're missing."

I got in my car and drove away, with him still standing there in the parking lot like he wasn't quite sure what had happened.

I DIDN'T CHECK my phone until I got to Mom's. No surprise, I had texts from Greg and Jackson. But I also had multiple missed calls and voicemails from Emerson. My heart gave a little leap when I saw his name on the screen, until I realized he was probably just calling to chew me out about investigating again.

Greg's text was professional but to the point—stay out of the investigation, it wasn't my place, I could be putting myself in danger.

Jackson just wanted me to loop him in on whatever I learned. I grinned when I read it. He was actually treating me like a partner of sorts. I liked it. It gave me a sense of closeness to Eileen, knowing that I was following in her footsteps and helping solve cases. I was proud to be her daughter and carry on her legacy in this small way.

Emerson's first voicemail was exactly what I expected. He was on the same wavelength as Greg, but less nice about it. His second voicemail sounded more panicked, with him telling me to call him as soon as I got the message.

I started to call him, but then stopped and put my phone away. We weren't together anymore. I didn't owe him any explanations.

And while I felt bad about him panicking, he would just have to learn to deal with that without my help. Neither one of us could move on if he still thought of himself as my protector.

MOM WAS STILL AWAKE, curled up in the living room, drinking a cup of hot tea and watching sitcom reruns when I got in.

"Waiting up for me?" I teased. "Did I make it before curfew?"

She smiled. "Maybe I was. How was your dinner?"

The guilt returned. "It was good," I said, dropping my purse and crashing on the couch across from her. "I wasn't totally open with you about the dinner," I admitted.

"I figured it was a date," she said. "I just don't know why you felt you had to hide that from me. It's not like you and Emerson were married. You're an adult, you're single, you can see who you want."

"That's not why I wasn't open."

"Oh?" She raised her eyebrows.

"I had dinner with Steve Wallace. He was the murder victim's research partner."

She leaned her head back, pressed her lips closed, then let out a loud sigh. "I see. So you're not just looking for the treasure, you're out chasing murderers again."

"No. Honest," I added when she raised her eyebrows again. "He's a historian as well, and I wanted more information about the treasure. What I found out was really interesting."

I started catching her up on everything Steve had told me about Annie Rogers and Harvey Logan, but was interrupted by yet another call from Emerson.

"Who is it?" Mom asked when she saw me roll my eyes and silence my phone again.

"It's Emerson. I texted Greg to let him know what I was doing tonight, and you know how tight those two are. Emerson started calling me just minutes after Greg texted to tell me to stay out of it."

"I think you should answer."

"I don't feel like getting lectured tonight. Besides, he can't have it both ways. He can't tell me what to do when we're barely even friends."

"Daphne, I don't know him as well as you, but he doesn't seem like the type to try to control you. He always seemed quite even-keeled when I was around him. If he's calling you multiple times, there may be a good reason. You need to find out what it is."

I sighed. She had a point, as much as I hated to admit it. "Fine. You're right. Let me just step out and call him."

I headed upstairs to the guest room, but he called again before I could get there. I didn't even have a chance to say hello before he cut me off, relief in his voice.

"Daphne. Thank God. I was afraid your phone was off."

"It was on silent. Listen, I know why you're calling."

"You do? I told them to let me be the one to tell you."

"Wait, what? Them who? What are you talking about?"

"Daphne—" He hesitated, and for the first time, I realized his voice still hadn't returned to normal. He had been relieved when I answered, but he was still strained. Something was terribly wrong.

"What is it?" Fear gripped me as I waited for him to answer.

"It's Fiona. She's in the hospital."

"The hospital?" Now I was truly panicked. "What happened? Is she okay?"

"I think she's going to be," he said, with way too much hesitation in his voice to make me feel better. "Apparently, she got one of her gut feelings that something was wrong at your place, and she had promised you she would look after it while you were gone. Instead of calling for help, she traipsed over by herself. She caught an intruder in the act."

"What?" I stopped where I was and sat down on the stairs, feeling like I was going to be sick. *Not Fiona.* My heart pounded. "What happened? Did he hurt her?"

"No," he said, chuckling. "She got the better of him, believe it or not. When she showed up brandishing her shotgun, he took off quickly. But Daphne, she's seventy-two years old. She had a heart attack."

"A heart attack? Fiona?" I couldn't believe it. Not her. She was so vital, so vibrant. I knew she was older, but her heart seemed as strong as a lion's. I couldn't fathom it betraying her that way.

"I know. I found her shortly after."

"How did you find her?"

"I went to her house to talk to her. The lights were on, but the back door was wide open, and she was nowhere to be found. I noticed fresh boot prints and followed them to the trail that leads from her house to yours."

"I'm so glad you were there." I closed my eyes and leaned my head against the wall. It was terrifying to think of Fiona alone and in pain. I was so grateful for whatever had taken Emerson to her doorstep that night.

"Me too. But listen, you're the closest thing she has to family. She would never ask you to come back early, you know that, but..."

"I'll leave first thing tomorrow," I said. I didn't even have to think about it. Fiona was more important than any investigation or treasure hunt.

"Good," he said, relief in his voice.

"How is she? I mean... She's going to make it, right?" I swallowed the lump in my throat.

"I think so, but we'll know more soon. She's in the cath lab now, getting stents placed. Joe and I are going to take turns staying with her until you get here."

"I'm so glad she's not alone. Thank you for being there."

"Of course," he said, his voice soft.

"And thank you for being the one to call and tell me."

"I know how much she means to you. I didn't want you to hear it from anyone else."

I gripped the phone and closed my eyes tightly. There were so many things I wanted to say. So many things I wanted to tell him. My heart ached so badly. I just wanted to be there now, to see that Fiona was okay, and to feel Emerson's arms around me, steadying me.

Life was short, even for someone as healthy and vibrant as Fiona.

Time would pass and life would move on, and someday it would be too late for second chances. It felt so wrong to feel so many things for someone, and to not even be able to say them. But I couldn't.

"Take care of her until I get there," I said, my voice strained.

Then I hung up the phone before I said anything else.

CHAPTER TWENTY-FOUR

Daphne

I LEFT BEFORE DAWN THE NEXT MORNING, ANXIOUS TO SEE Fiona for myself. I had to blink back tears anytime my mind drifted to her, picturing her alone and in pain on the floor at my house, or hooked up to wires in the hospital. I tried not to think of her at all, not while driving, but it was hard to think of anything else.

Mom had understood and had encouraged me to go, even though I could tell it disappointed her that our visit had been cut short. She agreed to postpone the upcoming estate sale and keep searching Dad's place for clues to the treasure. But I could tell she wished we were doing it together. I didn't blame her. That house held nothing but sad memories for her, and I hated putting her through that.

I drove faster than was strictly legal and made great time to the hospital, rushing straight to Fiona's room. When I walked in, she was sitting up, lecturing Joe about something as he sat by her bedside with a patient look on his face.

She was paler than normal, and my heart caught at how fragile she appeared sitting in that hospital bed. Even so, she was in better shape than I had feared. I let out a sigh of relief and leaned against the door, finally able to relax.

"Daphne, what on earth are you doing here?" she grumbled. "I hope you didn't rush back here on my account. I thought you'd be gone weeks longer."

"That was the plan," I said, walking to the chair Joe had vacated for me.

"Well, you shouldn't have let this ruin your plans. That's just ridiculous. A big fuss about nothing, if you ask me."

"Apparently, she was just napping at your house when Emerson found her," Joe said mildly, giving me a little wink.

"Napping?" I was utterly confused.

"Can't a woman take a rest when she needs to?" Fiona complained. "This is all just nonsense."

The doctor chose that moment to come into the room. Fiona immediately turned her irritation toward him. "When can I go home? I've got chickens waiting to be fed, young man."

"Now, Mrs. Flanagan—"

"That's *Miss* Flanagan, thank you very much."

"Yes, Miss Flanagan," the young doctor said, stumbling over the words. He pulled her chart from the wall and flipped through it quickly before walking over to her bedside. "I'm afraid we need to observe you a little longer. When someone of your age has a heart attack, even a mild—"

He broke off when Fiona slapped him across the face.

"What the—" His professionalism slipped as he held his cheek and stared at her in astonishment.

"How dare you say I had a heart attack," she said, giving him a meaningful look.

"But—" He started to protest until she held her hand up again in warning.

"I was *napping*," she said, overly enunciating the word. "And I won't have you worrying my friends here by saying anything otherwise."

"Y-yes ma'am." The man appeared petrified.

"And don't call me ma'am," she complained. "Treating me like an old woman. The nerve!"

Joe winked at me again. "Fiona, I'm going to take Daphne down to the cafeteria for some coffee," he said. "That way, you can talk to the doctor in private. Okay?"

She rolled her eyes and waved her hand in dismissal. I followed Joe's lead and stepped out of the room. We both died laughing the minute we hit the hallway.

"Well, she's her old self," I said, wiping a tear from my eyes.

"Don't let her fool you," he warned. "I was scared myself last night. It's a bigger deal than she'll admit. She thinks she's going to bust out of here and get right back to normal, but she's got a recovery ahead of her."

I shook my head, distraught. "So what happened at my house last night?"

"Let's walk," he said, guiding me down the hallway. "I wasn't kidding about the coffee. I haven't had a lick of sleep since it happened. Sheriff Morrison hasn't chosen to fill me in on the details, but what I gather is that there was an intruder at your house. Probably either thought you had the treasure there or the clues to it. Fiona confronted him by herself, of course."

He shook his head. The look on his face spoke of frustration mixed with admiration. "She ran him off. I gather the heart attack happened a few minutes later, after he was already gone. I haven't been to your house. The sheriff will want you to see if anything is missing. Emerson said your bookshelves were all a mess, but that's all he noticed while he was there."

"If he was looking through the books on my shelf, you're probably right about it being someone looking for clues to the treasure," I mused. "Otherwise, why not go straight upstairs for my jewelry? Or take the TV?"

He shook his head. "Not necessarily. Lots of people use false books to hide money and valuables. So I'm not basing my assumption on that. I'm basing it more on the rumors that have been flying around town."

I sighed. We reached the cafeteria, so I held off on asking my questions until he paid for his cup of coffee. I got one for myself, too, needing a hit of caffeine after my early morning.

When we were away from the crowd of people and alone again in the hallway, I asked, "More rumors than you already told me?"

"The story gets bigger every time someone tells it," he said in that calm tone that annoyed me to death. "You're the talk of the town. Everyone's talking about how you moved back here and paid full price in cash for that house, even though it was filthy and hadn't been updated in years. Rumor has it Lonnie made off with millions, stolen right out from under Bill Brinksley's nose, and that he buried part of it somewhere on your property. Supposedly, that's why you came back here and bought that house—so you could dig it up. I've heard lots of other things too. You know how people here talk." He rolled his eyes. "Some people think the treasure was never found, but that Lonnie gave you the clues to it, and you're here looking for it. If you thought you were famous before, you're an even bigger sensation now." He chuckled.

I groaned. "But for all the wrong reasons."

"That's the way it usually works," he said, shrugging.

"Did Fiona get a look at the intruder?"

"Probably. Unfortunately, she can't remember what happened leading up to her so-called nap."

"I see." I let out a breath. "So we've got nothing on who did this."

"I wouldn't say that yet. When you go home, keep your eyes open. Keep your other senses open." He shot me a meaningful look. "You never know. Maybe you'll get something."

We made it back to Fiona's door, but he stopped me from going in.

"Catch me up on what you found out in Arkansas," he said. "I don't want Fiona getting all worked up about it."

I filled him in on what I had learned from Steve Wallace.

He whistled in appreciation. "Kid Curry himself! Now that makes it even more fun." He let out a rare grin. "I hope it's true, and I hope we get to see the treasure for ourselves."

"You're a former sheriff. Don't tell me you're going all fanboy over an outlaw," I teased.

He shrugged. "You and I both know I've got a little outlaw in me. I think we all do. Another life and I may have chosen a very different path than I did in this one." A quick look of pain floated across his face. I knew he was thinking of the mistake that still haunted him.

"Maybe so. But the important thing is that you did choose the good in this one. Everyone makes mistakes sometimes," I said gently.

He cleared his throat and changed the subject. "Are you good to stay with Fiona for a bit? I could use a shower and a nap if you can hang out here."

"Of course."

"Alright." He opened the door and followed me into the room. The doctor had gone, and Fiona was sleeping peacefully.

"When she wakes up, tell her I'm going to take care of her chickens," Joe whispered. "She'll worry about them."

"Okay. Thanks, Joe." I squeezed his hand as he left and closed the door gently behind him. He cared for Fiona more than he would admit. Considering how well they got along, it surprised me that nothing had ever come of it. I couldn't imagine what they were waiting for at their ages.

I FOUND an extra blanket and curled up in the recliner beside Fiona's bed. I needed a nap and figured I should sleep while she did. I had just dozed off when a light knock on the door woke me.

"Come in," I called softly, trying not to wake Fiona.

Emerson stepped into the room carrying a vase of wildflowers. He stopped suddenly, looking shocked to see me there. My heart flip-flopped in my chest. I wanted nothing more than to run to him, to feel his arms wrapped around me, to hear him tell me everything was really going to be okay. But the distance between us was as real as if someone had put a barrier in place.

"I didn't think you would be here yet," he said, as if apologizing for his presence.

"I got up early and drove fast." I rose from the recliner and took the flowers from him. My fingers lightly brushed his as I did. It felt like electricity shot through my body, nearly overwhelming me.

I turned my back to him and put the flowers on the table beside Fiona's bed, hiding my face until I recovered. "Those are perfect. She'll love them."

"How is she?"

I gestured for him to follow me out into the hallway. We closed the door softly to avoid waking her.

"She slapped the doctor for saying she had a heart attack," I said, raising an eyebrow.

He grinned. "So she's going to be okay then."

"I think so, yeah. They're just monitoring her now. Hopefully, she'll get to go home soon. You know how she hates it here."

"She'll be really glad you're here with her," he said, looking at me intently. "You know you're family to her."

"I know. She's my family too." I meant it. She was the closest thing I had to a grandmother, and even though I couldn't remember it, she had known me since I was born. We may not have been blood, but our bond was as strong as any family.

"Listen, can we talk? I have some things I—" He frowned and stopped talking, looking behind me.

"Hey, Daphne," a familiar voice called out.

I turned around to see Jackson's grin.

"Glad you made it safe," he said. "Joe told me I could find you here. Do you have a few minutes to talk about the break-in at your house?"

"Sure," I said. "Give me just a minute."

I turned back to Emerson, but he was already gone.

CHAPTER TWENTY-FIVE

Daphne

I TURNED BACK TO JACKSON, STIFLING A SIGH. "WELL, I guess I'm free right now." I forced a small smile.

"Great! I just wanted to give you an update. We'll need you to check out your house as quickly as possible, look things over, and tell us if anything is missing. If you claim anything on insurance, you'll need the official report. You can come in tomorrow morning to file it. Your back door lock is busted, so you'll want to get that changed right away. And if you see additional damage, let us know."

I nodded. "Okay. I'm not sure when I'll be heading back there, though. I'm going to stay with Fiona here until she's released."

"Understood," he said, nodding. "Just let me know when you get there and have time to look over anything. Unfortunately, Fiona was the only witness, and she doesn't remember much. We dusted for prints, but I'll be honest with you, the odds of us getting a hit off that are low, and this isn't going to be a high priority for the crime lab. It could be months before we hear anything."

"So we may never find out who it was?"

He nodded. "Unfortunately."

"Great." I covered my face with my hands and let out a deep breath. "I feel like all I've done is cause trouble since I moved here. I'm sorry."

"Hey, that's not the way I see it," he said. "You're not the one causing all of this. You may be the one getting the short end of all of it, though."

"No, not even. Fiona is lying there in a hospital bed because she was trying to protect my house." The thought of it made me furious. "If I were the only one suffering, that would be one thing. But this?" I lifted my hands helplessly. "I can't stand it, Jackson."

"Hey, I know." His face sobered, maybe for the first time since all this had started. "Everyone loves Fiona, and we're all upset about what happened. But the intruder didn't hurt her. She's an elderly lady whose heart acted up. If it didn't happen then, it would have happened somewhere else."

"I know that, logically. But—" my voice broke, and I couldn't continue.

"Hey, hey, hey, it's all going to be okay." He had an awkward expression on his face, as if he wasn't sure how to deal with my emotional display. He cleared his throat and reminded me to come in the next day to file that report, then patted me on the shoulder and left.

Once again, I found myself wishing that Emerson was there and mine to lean on. But he wasn't.

The only person I had to lean on was myself.

I LINGERED in the hallway for a minute, still hoping Emerson would return. But it soon became clear that he had really left. Again. So I sighed, gave up, and headed back into Fiona's room. I found her awake with a scowl on her face.

I took the chair beside her. "I'm sorry I woke you."

"I've had plenty of rest," she grumbled. "In fact, if I don't get out of here soon, I'm going to plumb rot in this bed."

I patted her hand. "It's hard for you to be stuck here, isn't it?"

"You better believe it, missy."

She opened her mouth to speak again, but we were interrupted by yet another doctor.

"Good news, Ms. Flanagan!" he said, greeting her with a bright smile before she could growl at him. "You've been completely stable since surgery, and the team agrees you can go home to finish your recuperation. We'll have some instructions, of course, as well as some medications you'll need to start taking, and you'll need to be followed carefully for some time. But it's safe enough for you to be discharged now. I think we all agree you'll bounce back faster in your own home."

Fiona breathed a giant sigh of relief. "Glory be! Come on, Daphne, let's bust this joint."

"Are you sure?" I asked the doctor, worried. "Is it typical to get released that quickly after this type of event?"

He nodded. "I assure you, we wouldn't let her go if we were concerned. Twelve to twenty-four hours is standard procedure. She's recovering beautifully already, and morale plays a role in recovery times. She'll need to take it easy for a few days, but I'm confident she'll be just fine."

I leaned my head back and let out a sigh of relief. A weight lifted off my chest, and I smiled for the first time in what felt like ages.

Fiona was already starting to remove her own IV. The doctor stopped her with a laugh and asked her to please let the nurses do it instead.

"They need the practice, you know," he said, with a wink to me that Fiona couldn't see.

She grumbled but agreed to sit tight, settling down a bit now that the light at the end of the tunnel was in sight.

I packed up her things quickly, and the nursing staff put a rush on her release. I had a feeling she hadn't been the easiest patient, and they were all as ready for her to go home as she was. We only had a short wait before they had the discharge paperwork ready, her medication bagged up, and a wheelchair waiting for me to push her out to my car. They could have saved themselves a little more time by skipping the wheelchair—no way was Fiona Flanagan going to leave the hospital that way. She would walk out on her own two feet even if it killed her, though truth be told, she seemed to have gained all her old strength back after being told she could leave. I silently gave a prayer of thanks for the doctor's wisdom in letting her finish her recovery at home. He was right. It was where she needed to be.

I carried her things and walked with her out to my car so I could drive her home. With every step, my anxiety grew, but I didn't know why. We needed to leave, but I couldn't shake the feeling that something terrible was going to happen.

I shook myself, realizing that my feelings were probably nothing more than a touch of PTSD. After all, just a few weeks prior, I had been released from this exact same hospital—and had driven straight into the trap my would-be killer had waiting for me at home.

It's not the same, I reassured myself. *This is just anxiety, not a premonition. You're okay. Everything is going to be fine.*

But my body didn't believe me.

Chapter Twenty-Six

Emerson

I walked away from Daphne the minute she turned toward Jackson. I didn't even think about it. It was an automatic reaction to seeing them together, to knowing I didn't belong in that picture.

I had missed my chance.

He had come running as soon as she arrived in town. She had probably called him to let him know she was almost there.

I saw the way his face lit up when he saw her standing there.

A wave of regret washed over me.

I climbed into my truck, but I couldn't force myself to drive away. I felt stuck. I leaned my forehead against the steering wheel and groaned.

I knew I should walk away for a million different reasons. Daphne would be better off with Jackson. No matter how much I currently disliked him, he had to be a decent guy. After all, Greg trusted him implicitly. Plus, he had shown up here at the hospital for Daphne's sake. I knew he wasn't there for Fiona.

And while all I wanted was to let go of the promise to my brother and win Daphne back, I knew deep down that I was still bound to it.

Just because I wanted to let go didn't mean I could. I had looked into my brother's eyes, gripped his hand, and given my word. No, he hadn't asked for it. But I had given it just the same.

"I wish you were here, Ken." I spoke the words aloud, my voice breaking as I said his name. Hot tears came even though I tried to force them back.

"Man, I wish you were here. Nothing's the same without you. *I'm not the same without you.*"

My throat ached, but I kept talking anyway. The words wouldn't stop even if I tried to hold them back. I had kept everything inside for so long. I'd even remained stoic at his funeral. It had been my duty. I had to be strong for Mom, Dad, Alex, and Sarah. But now, everything I felt was coming up, and I couldn't bury it anymore. I needed to feel it, needed to say it.

I needed to say goodbye.

"You were my best friend." My voice broke again. "And I'm sorry. I'm so, so sorry Ken."

The tears flowed freely. Tears for Ken and for the future he lost. Tears for Sarah and the love she still grieved.

Tears for me. For the loss of the best friend I'd ever had.

It was the first time I had allowed myself to cry. It hurt like hell, and it felt like it would never end.

But when the tears finally eased, I could feel that they had washed away some of the grief. It was still there. But it was lighter. Bearable.

"I wish... I wish I had some kind of sign that it was okay for me to let go of that promise." I felt stupid even saying the words. I didn't believe in signs, and I didn't believe Ken could hear me, much less give me one.

I put the keys into my truck's ignition, started the engine, and put it in reverse. My phone dinged.

I put the truck back in park and picked up my phone to look at the text. It was from Mom.

I have great news. Sarah met someone. She came over to tell me today. She was so worried about what I would think—isn't that silly? I told her I was overjoyed for her. Ken loved her. He wouldn't want her to grieve forever. That's not the kind of man he was. He would want her to love and be loved and have a happy life.

I stared at the text in disbelief. Another one came through, just one line this time.

He would want the same for you, you know.

Tears came again, and I didn't even try to stop them. Maybe I would start believing in signs after all.

"Thanks, Ken," I whispered, my voice raw.

I pulled the keys out of my truck and headed back into the hospital to find Daphne.

I JOGGED up the stairs to the hospital's third floor with a lighter heart than I had felt in years. I still missed my brother. That would never go away. But something inside me had changed. I felt free. I had my brother's blessing to move on with my life, and I was lucky enough to have found the woman I wanted to spend it with. I only hoped I wasn't too late. If she wanted Jackson, I would stand by and wish them well, no matter how much it hurt. But I had seen the look in her eyes when our fingers touched in Fiona's room. It made me think there had to at least be a chance.

I sped down the hallway to Fiona's door only to find it open. Her bed was empty, and housekeeping was already working on her room. I detoured to the nurses' station to ask about her.

"Oh, she got released. Thank goodness," Beth, the nurse at the desk, said. She gave me a knowing look.

I grinned. "Was she a handful?"

"And a half. Dr. Lewis will never be the same."

"It will be good for him." I grinned again. It was fun, feeling light-hearted and free.

"Exactly." Beth giggled. She paused and bit her bottom lip nervously before changing gears. "Ah, Emerson, I've been meaning to ask... Would you like to have coffee sometime? We've run into each other so many times through work that I feel like I know you, but, well, I'd love to get to know you better." She shot me a shy smile.

I was caught off guard. On one hand, Beth wasn't like the women of Rosemary Mountain who had treated me like nothing more than fresh meat when I'd arrived. She was nice, and I was flattered.

But my heart was spoken for.

It was Daphne's. Even if she had moved on, even if she didn't want it, even if I had to watch her be happy with someone else. There was only one woman I had any interest in having coffee with, no matter how nice Beth was.

"Thanks," I said. "I'm flattered, really. But—"

"You don't have to explain," she said, holding up a hand. "I know you're not really the dating type. I just thought you seemed happier tonight, and well, like you were enjoying talking to me..."

"I was. It's not you. Really. It's just that, well, I'm sort of taken."

"Sort of?" She gave me a weird look. "I thought you and Daphne broke up?"

"We did. It's complicated. I'm not sure I could explain it even if I tried. We aren't together, but I'm going to try to win her back." I grinned again, feeling it light up my whole face. "You're the first person I've told that to, and that's probably awful since you just asked me out, but you're right that I'm happier tonight, and she's the reason. I can't help it. I'm sorry."

"Don't be," she said with a genuine smile. "It's good to see you happy. I hope you win her back."

"I do too."

Man, I hoped I hadn't screwed things up permanently.

I DROVE straight to Daphne's house. She wasn't there, which made sense. She was probably still getting Fiona settled in. I debated between waiting on her front porch or going to Fiona's myself, but in the end, I chose another path. Daphne's lock hadn't been repaired yet. That was something I could do for her, and selfishly, I would sleep a lot better that night knowing she had a working lock, even if our conversation didn't go the way I hoped.

So I got in my truck and headed back toward Rosemary Mountain, hoping I could make it to the hardware store and back before she left Fiona's.

Chapter Twenty-Seven

Daphne

I TRIED MY BEST TO SHAKE OFF MY NEGATIVE FEELINGS AND to be bright and happy for Fiona's sake. She was overjoyed at the prospect of going home. I reassured her that Joe had taken care of her chickens and that we would both help out over the next few days while she recovered, so she didn't need to worry about anything. Of course, that was the wrong thing to say. She was just fine, thank you very much, and didn't need us messing up her kitchen or anything else just to make ourselves feel better.

She was definitely back to her old self.

I was deeply grateful for it. I knew things could have been so much worse. Fiona might have been feeling better, but I was still terrified about how close a call it had been.

All of Emerson's words about me putting people in danger came flooding back, and I felt worse with every passing mile.

Fiona's face lit up when we finally pulled into her driveway. But I still couldn't quite relax.

I carried the flowers Emerson had brought her inside and put them on her kitchen table. "I know you said you didn't need me messing around in your kitchen, but would you like me to make you dinner? I can also stay here tonight, if you want, just to be sure..."

She rolled her eyes. "Thank you, dear, but I'm starving and we both know you aren't much of a cook. And I don't need you babysitting me. I've been taking care of myself for quite some time, you know."

"I know," I said with a small laugh. It was clear she was ready for me to leave, but I couldn't bring myself to. Not yet. I stood at the doorway fiddling with the zipper of my coat, wishing she would ask me to stay.

The truth was, I wanted to stay partly for selfish reasons. I didn't want to admit it to her, but it scared me to go back home, knowing what had happened there. Since I hadn't yet called someone to change the lock for me, I wasn't even sure I could secure the door properly.

I knew if I told Fiona these things, she would immediately invite me to stay. But I could also see that, after her hospital stay, she was feeling annoyed with people and just wanted to get back to her normal routine. I could understand that. And I knew if I stayed with her, she would think she had to cook for me and take care of me. I couldn't do that to her while she was still weak and recovering.

So I hugged her tightly and told her to call me if she needed anything, then left to face my broken cottage alone.

DESPITE ALL MY WORRIES, I couldn't help but smile as I turned out of Fiona's driveway and headed home. Even after everything, this mountain was still my favorite place on earth. It held a piece of my soul, somehow, and coming back here truly felt like coming home.

Emerson's truck was sitting in my driveway, but he was nowhere in sight. I hopped out of my car and walked around back, where I found him changing my broken lock.

"Oh, hey," he said, looking up. "I'm almost finished here. I took pictures of the damage. I'll text them to you."

I walked to him. "You didn't have to do this. But thank you," I said quietly. "I was nervous about sleeping here tonight without a proper lock. It was really nice of you to think of this."

He looked down at me, his eyes full of so many unsaid things. He started to speak, but stopped. He reached up and brushed his fingertips along my cheek, then leaned down and placed his lips on mine.

The kiss was soft, hesitant, as if he was unsure it would be welcome. A single tear ran down my cheek as I leaned into him, deepening the kiss, trying somehow to tell him everything in my heart without saying a word.

He brushed my cheek again and broke the kiss, pulling me into his arms. "I missed you so much," he whispered.

"I missed you, too," I whispered back, hoping we both meant the same thing.

"Have you had dinner?"

"No. Not yet."

He pulled back and looked at me. "I know you need to look around and check things out here. But after that, would you have dinner with me?"

"Yes." I nodded. I didn't think twice before answering, didn't even stop to consider how odd this whole thing was.

He smiled, relief evident, then turned back to my lock. I stood watching, feeling completely off balance. The man was an enigma. Before I left for Arkansas, he told me we could never be together. Now, he was kissing me and inviting me to dinner like nothing had ever happened.

And what annoyed me more than anything was that all it took was one kiss to make me melt into his arms.

"That should do it," he said, standing back to look at his work. "Here's your new key." He handed it to me.

"Thanks. Really. I really appreciate it."

"Sure thing." He grinned at me, reminding me of the Emerson I'd known before he went back to Wisconsin.

The Emerson I'd fallen in love with.

"Do you want to come in with me?" I asked, feeling oddly shy. "If you have time, you can hang out while I look things over, then we can go to dinner together."

"Of course." He opened the door and gestured for me to go in first. "After you."

I walked into the cottage and frowned. The energy felt off, wrong somehow. Like I could still feel traces of the intruder's presence.

Once again, my safe haven had been violated, and I hated it.

"Doesn't look like he did too much damage," Emerson commented.

"No."

I sighed. I wouldn't try to explain to Emerson that the real damage couldn't be seen.

A few books had been knocked off my shelves, and a lamp had been knocked over, probably while the intruder was running away from Fiona. But other than that, everything seemed in order. I checked my jewelry and the other rooms in the house, just in case, but there was no sign that he had even made it out of the living room. The rest of the house felt as it should, with nothing out of place.

"Well, that's easy enough," I said. "Just let me change and freshen up a bit before we go to dinner. Where do you have in mind?"

"Actually, I was hoping you would come to my cabin. I thought I would cook for you." He stuck his hands into his pockets and leaned back, nervous as he waited for my reaction.

I had never been to his house before. The opportunity had never come up during the short time we'd dated. I knew, based on his personality, that it was his sanctuary, the same way the cottage was mine. Being invited there felt like he was opening the door for something new, something deeper between us. Which didn't make sense, considering everything he'd said the last time we had talked. But I was honored, just the same.

"That sounds nice," I said with a shy smile. "I'll be ready in just a minute."

I went back upstairs and changed out of my worn traveling clothes into a fresh sweater and jeans. I felt the thrill of butterflies, even as I warned myself not to get my hopes up.

The last thing I wanted was to have them dashed into the ground again.

Chapter Twenty-Eight

Emerson held the door to his truck open for me, and I climbed in, just like old times. My emotions were a swirling mix of confusion. Something was different. *He* was different. Or was I just getting my hopes up again?

If there was one thing I knew about him, it was that he had a bit of a savior complex. And here I was, again, in need of saving. It was just like him to show up and fix my lock. It was even like him to want to stick close by, to keep me safe in case the intruder tried again.

But it was also like him to walk away as soon as the danger was over.

I promised myself to remember that, to not get caught up in thinking things were different this time.

Still, something had changed. It seemed like some of the pain he'd carried had disappeared. He was lighter, happier, more like the version of himself I had met when I first came to Rosemary Mountain. I couldn't help but be curious about it.

We drove to the turnoff for his cabin in friendly silence. It felt as if we were both unsure of what to say, but somehow, it wasn't awkward.

In fact, I felt more relaxed than I had in a long time, like everything was finally right in the world again.

As we pulled into his driveway, the first snowflakes of the year began to fall, thick, heavy snowflakes that promised to stick. I sat up eagerly and watched with delight. He put the truck in park but didn't make a move to get out. When I glanced over, I found him watching me with a smile on his face.

"What?" I asked.

"It's just nice to see you so happy," he said.

The butterflies in my stomach betrayed me, starting their dance yet again and defying the promises I had just made to myself.

Emerson hopped out of the truck and came around to open my door for me. His fingertips automatically came to the small of my back as he guided me to the front door of his cabin, starting an internal war within me. What on earth was I doing? This man had no intention whatsoever of having a future with me, so why was I putting myself in this position? Why was I letting him smile at me, touch me, *kiss* me, when it was inevitably going to lead to my own heartbreak?

I shouldn't be here. I should go home.

But I couldn't seem to force myself to walk away.

When he opened the front door of the log cabin, his beautiful German Shepherd was waiting for him. The dog's face lit up, his body vibrating with anticipation as he sat waiting for Emerson's command.

"This is Thor," Emerson said, flashing that grin I loved so much. "You haven't met him properly yet. Thor, this is Daphne. She's a friend. You can say hi."

Thor walked to me and sniffed my hand, his tail wagging. I patted him on his head and scratched behind his ears. In return, he daintily licked my hand, a solemn look on his gorgeous face.

"He likes you," Emerson said. "Not everyone gets Thor kisses."

"He's a sweetie," I said, already in love. "And really well-behaved."

"He's had a lot of training. Here, let me take your coat."

I shrugged off the heavy winter coat and gave it to Emerson, who hung it in the closet by the front door. I tore my attention away from

Thor and glanced around the cabin, curious. It was surprisingly neat and had a warm feeling to it. It was masculine and sparsely decorated, but even so, it felt like a nice place to be. Emerson had chosen quality wood furniture and a nice leather sofa. There was a stack of books beside what appeared to be his favorite chair, and a neat pile of logs beside the wood-burning fireplace. It was a cozy place and smelled of cedar and sandalwood. Just like him.

"I told you once that I could cook if I put my mind to it," he said, breaking me out of my thoughts. "I guess it's time to put that to the test." He grinned and took my hand, leading me to the kitchen.

It was masculine too, with no decoration at all, but it was fresh and clean. He opened his refrigerator and took a look, contemplating.

"I guess I should have planned this out better," he admitted. "It was kind of a spur-of-the-moment thing. How do you feel about spaghetti?"

"Spaghetti's fine," I answered. "But, out of curiosity, since this obviously wasn't planned, why did you invite me over?"

He paused and looked back at me. "Well, I wanted to talk. I wanted to tell you some things."

"So tell me."

"It's not as easy to talk about as I thought it would be," he admitted, turning away to pull ingredients out of the refrigerator. "It may take me a little time to find the right words."

"Or maybe you shouldn't worry about finding the 'right' words, and should just tell me what's going on," I suggested.

He nodded. "That's fair."

He opened a cabinet door, pulled out a cutting board, and began chopping up an onion. "Well, it's like this," he said, avoiding my eyes. "I know I told you before about my brother and the promise I made to him."

"Right..."

"Well, you and Fiona were both right. That promise didn't do anything to help my brother. It was just keeping me miserable. I was punishing myself out of guilt."

I stayed silent, wanting to give him the space to say what was obviously difficult for him to talk about. It was clear he was struggling to find the right words and that he was uncomfortable. At the same time, I was dying for him to just spill whatever he wanted to say. No matter how many silent admonishments I gave myself, my hopes were growing by the second. But my fears were, too. I was afraid he was going to tell me he had decided we could date as long as we kept it casual and understood there was no future there. And that, I knew, would never work for me.

"Anyway," he continued, "I've been kind of dealing with that grief. Fiona gave me some tea. I don't know how or why it works, but—"

"But it does," I interrupted with a small laugh. "Fiona's given me tea before, too. She knows what she's doing."

"Yeah." He grinned again and raised his eyebrows, finally meeting my gaze. "I'm man enough to admit when I'm wrong, and I guess I've been wrong about a lot of things lately, Fiona included. Look, I know this sounds crazy, but I think my brother sent me a sign that it's okay to let go of that promise."

The words came out in a rush, as if he was worried I would think *he* was crazy. Which was funny, considering how I was usually the one on that end of our conversations.

"That's great, Emerson," I said sincerely. "I'm really happy you're feeling better." I kept my words focused on him and his healing, even as my heart beat a little faster, hoping.

"Yeah." He put down the knife and walked over to where I was. He pulled out a chair and sat down across from me. Our knees touched as he looked directly into my eyes.

"Look," he said, "I know I screwed things up with us. And I know I don't deserve a second chance. But I've missed you. Daphne, I've missed you every single moment of every single day we've been apart. I've never felt this way about anyone—ever." He took my hand in his and continued gazing at me with earnest eyes that begged me to believe him. "I've told myself to back off, that Jackson's better for you and I shouldn't get in the way, that—"

"Wait, what?" I interrupted, confused. "Jackson? What are you talking about?"

"I know he's younger than me, happier than me, less, well, *broken* than me. He's good for you, and if you choose him, I'll respect that. I hurt you, and I understand if it's too late to make that right. But, I don't know, I thought maybe if we talked, maybe if you came over for dinner, well, maybe…"

"Maybe what?" My heart beat so quickly as I waited to hear the words I longed for.

"It's stupid. I know we can't just pick up where we left off." He groaned and ran a hand through his hair. "But we were good together, and I just thought maybe if we had dinner, you might remember the good. Dammit, Daphne, I love you, and—"

"You love me?" I whispered, my eyes wide.

He looked startled, like he hadn't expected those words to come out. He paused for a moment before speaking again. "Yeah, I do. I love you. I think I have since the day I met you. I tried to stop. First, because of my brother, and second, because of you and Jackson. You deserve better than me. But I've already racked up so many regrets in my life, I needed to tell you how I feel. It's selfish, I know, when you've probably already moved on. Forgive me for that. But I do love you. I'm sorry I didn't tell you sooner. I'm sorry for all the ways I screwed this up. Like I said, I'll respect it if you tell me to get lost. I just had to try."

I was momentarily speechless. He stared at me, waiting for me to speak, with eyes that seemed afraid to hope.

"Emerson, I love you too." The words came out softly, shyly. His face changed as the weight of them sank in.

I reached up and stroked his beard, reassuring him. He rested his face in my hand and kissed my palm. "And there's nothing at all between me and Jackson," I continued. "I don't even know where you got that idea. I love *you*. I want *you*. Only you."

He stood up and pulled me to him in reply, grazing my cheek with his fingertips as he looked deep into my eyes. For a moment, time seemed to stand still. Then his lips found mine in a kiss that felt unlike any we'd shared before, a kiss that was full of love and promise.

He finally broke the kiss but pulled me even closer, resting his head on mine as I sank into his embrace.

"So it's not too late?" he whispered against my hair.

"Never. Not for us."

CHAPTER TWENTY-NINE

Daphne

I COULD HAVE STAYED IN EMERSON'S ARMS ALL NIGHT, BUT he had promised to cook me dinner and he was determined to do so. I felt oddly shy sitting in his kitchen while he put together the spaghetti. The whole thing seemed surreal, and yet, at the same time, more real than anything else in my whole life.

He asked me to catch him up on the case while he cooked, which surprised me since he had discouraged me from being part of it at all. But I supposed the break-in at my house had changed things. I was involved in a way that he couldn't deny now. It had touched my life, my home. Because he loved me, he was as invested as I was in finding out the truth about the treasure—and about Wesley's killer.

He listened quietly while I told him about having dinner with Steve and what Joe had shared regarding Lonnie and Bill Brinksley.

"I don't like that at all," he said. "I guess I'm out of the loop on gossip right now, but if the whole town thinks you've got a line on the treasure, then it could have been anyone breaking into your house."

"I know. It's frustrating. And unless we actually find the gold, I'm not sure how to clear Dad's name. Worse, I'm not totally certain Bill's wrong," I admitted.

He poured me a glass of wine and sat across from me, putting his hand over mine. "We'll figure it out."

A little of the weight on my shoulders fell off, knowing that he was truly in this with me.

"I have to file the police report tomorrow morning," I said. "Do you want to come with me?"

"Sure," he agreed. "And after that, what if we go back to the scene of the crime? See if we can find anything there."

"You want to investigate with me?" I asked, a grin forming.

He winked. "Somebody's gotta keep an eye on you."

The inner voice of doubt reminded me of his savior complex, but I tried my very best to ignore her. I didn't want her ruining things.

"I think the spaghetti's ready," Emerson said, apparently not noticing the flicker of doubt on my face. "Listen, we can eat here at the table, of course. Or, we could recreate that date at your cottage and eat in front of the fire."

He smiled at me, and the doubts melted away again. He remembered the night of our first kiss. How could I doubt that?

"That sounds nice," I said, returning his smile.

"Great. I'll get a fire going." He hopped up and gave me a quick kiss before heading into the living room. I made myself at home in the kitchen, finding plates and silverware for our dinner. By the time he had a fire blazing, I had carried our little picnic to the fireplace hearth.

"Look outside," he said, pointing at his back windows. He had pulled back the flannel curtains, revealing a magical scene. At least an inch of snow had already fallen onto his back porch. Further out, his barn light shone, a hazy glow illuminating the falling snow. It was beautiful, and I felt so happy and grateful to share it with him.

"I've just got to go lock up the chickens real quick," he said. "Then I'll be back."

"You have chickens?" I knew he had mentioned animals, plural, but we had never talked specifics.

"Yeah. A couple dozen of them," he said, laughing. "They will have already put themselves up for the night, but I've got to make sure the door to the coop is secure. Don't want any predators going after them."

"Can I come with you?"

"Sure." He grinned. "Grab your coat."

I bundled up quickly in my coat and gloves and followed him out into the falling snow. He took my hand and led me across the yard, shining a flashlight to lead the way. To my surprise, we didn't head toward the barn at all, but to a smaller chicken coop I hadn't even spotted in the dark.

"I'm going to peek in and make sure they're all home," he said quietly before opening the door. He kept the flashlight low, to not spook them, and did a quick count. "Yep, they're all here. Want to see?"

"Yeah," I said, although I was a bit nervous. I had only seen Fiona's chickens at a distance and wasn't quite sure how these might react to a stranger poking her head inside their home at night. I took a quick peek and saw they were all lined up on a high roosting bar, settled in nice and cozy.

I pulled my head back out so Emerson could close and lock the door to the coop. "Won't they get cold?" I asked.

"No, not at these temps. They're hardier than they look, and the deep litter straw keeps the coop warm in the winter."

"You take good care of them," I commented.

He stopped and looked down at me with a tender smile. "I always take care of what's mine."

He leaned down and kissed me, while snow swirled around us, making me feel as if we were the only two people in this whole, beautiful world.

After being out in the cold, the warmth of the fire felt especially welcoming. I left my boots by the door with my snow-covered coat and sat cross-legged in front of the fireplace

It was hard to believe that just twenty-four hours ago I had been in Little Rock on a fake date with a man I couldn't stand, believing there was no chance for a future with Emerson. Things had changed so much, in so many ways, in such a short time.

Which, come to think about it, had been my experience ever since moving to Rosemary Mountain. One thing was certain. Life here was never stagnant. The mountain herself changed dramatically each season, and life here somehow seemed to reflect that. It was a bit unnerving. But at least this time, the change was one that made me incredibly happy.

"How's the pasta?" Emerson asked.

"Surprisingly good," I answered.

"Surprisingly?" His brows rose.

I giggled. "Well, I wasn't sure whether to believe you when you said you knew how to cook. But you have me beat for sure."

He grinned again.

Though we'd both doubted whether we could pick up where we had left off, it seemed we had done just that. After dinner, we curled up on the couch with the rest of the bottle of wine and fell into easy conversation. He told me about his family and all about his visit with them, sharing more than he ever had. I opened up to him about my mixed feelings about Janet and my dad and how confusing everything had been since Dad's death.

I finally yawned, feeling the fatigue of such a long day, and glanced at my watch. "I had no idea it was so late!" I exclaimed. I was astonished to see it was already midnight.

Emerson looked at his own watch, his eyes showing surprise as well. "Me either, actually." He looked out the back window and frowned. "Daphne, I'll try to drive you home if that's what you want. But why don't you stay here tonight?"

My eyes widened. He immediately put up his hands in response.

"I'll be a perfect gentleman," he said with a little smile playing on his lips. "I'm not trying to rush you into anything you aren't ready for. But I think we got more snow than they were calling for, and we might have some trouble getting up to your cottage. On top of that, there's still a killer on the loose, and well, I'd feel a lot better about you staying here. You can take my bed and I'll sleep on the couch. If you're not comfortable with that, though, I'll put some chains on my tires and we'll give it a go."

I hesitated and bit my lip. I was happy to stay with him. But I wasn't so sure I wanted him to be a perfect gentleman. On one hand, we had just gotten back together, and considering our history, it would be wise to take things slow. On the other hand, if there was one thing Rosemary Mountain had taught me, it was that life could change dramatically—or even end—at any moment.

I loved Emerson. And he loved me. We had been drawn to each other from the moment we'd met in a way I couldn't possibly describe. It felt like my whole life had been leading me to him, and him to me.

And knowing that, it felt silly to wait.

"I'll stay," I said, feeling shy again. My heart pounded, this time with anticipation.

"Good," he said, smiling. He took my glass and the empty bottle and carried them to the kitchen, then came back to me.

"I'll show you my room," he said. "And I'll find you some sweats or something to sleep in. They'll be too big on you, but at least you'll be warm."

He took my hand and led me down the hallway to his bedroom. Like the rest of the cabin, it was sparsely decorated, but was neat and clean.

"The bathroom is in there," he said, pointing to a door in the corner as he pulled open one of his drawers. "And here's something that should work for you to sleep in." He handed me a folded pair of sweatpants and a long-sleeve T-shirt. "I'll let you get some sleep. Hopefully, the road will be clear in the morning."

He started to walk away, but I grabbed his hand. When he turned back to me, I said just two words.

"Emerson... Stay."

He looked at me with a question on his face. In answer, I put the sweats on top of his dresser and stepped closer, putting my arms around his neck.

"Stay," I whispered again.

"Are you sure?" His voice was a whisper, too.

I nodded and brushed his lips with mine.

"I love you, Daphne," he said.

"I love you, too, Emerson." The words were still new, yet somehow felt right and familiar, like I had just been waiting all this time to say it.

He pulled me close and held me for just a moment before lifting me. I wrapped my legs around his waist, and he carried me to his bed.

Chapter Thirty

Emerson

I woke to find Daphne curled up against me, sleeping peacefully with her red hair spread across my chest. So it hadn't just been a dream. She had given me another chance, had chosen to forgive and start over. It was more than I'd expected. More than I deserved. I was a lucky man, and I promised myself I would show her just how much I loved her, every single day for the rest of our lives.

The rest of our lives.

The thought hit me like a ton of bricks. I knew what I wanted—a future. Marriage. Kids. But was that what she wanted? She had taken me back so sweetly, but I had to remind myself that she and I were two very different people in two very different life stages.

I was thirty-two, settled, and had already sewn my wild oats. I had no interest in casual dating. Last night had meant something to me. For me, it was a commitment, something I took very seriously.

But Daphne was barely out of college and had proven to be pretty independent. She was already flitting back and forth from here to Little Rock, and Fiona had told me she was still considering moving back to

Arkansas. She said she loved me, but did that mean the same thing to her as it did to me?

All these thoughts were making me uncomfortable, so I told myself to stop being such a, well, *girl* about the whole thing. I loved her. If she wanted me, I was here. If not, well, I'd employ every skill I had to convince her otherwise. That thought put a grin on my face, and I immediately went to work doing just that, using my free hand to stroke her back.

"Mmm..." she said, slowly opening her sleepy eyes. "Good morning."

"Good morning, beautiful." I tipped her chin toward me and kissed her. Yes, I would enjoy convincing her that settling down with me wouldn't be the worst thing in the world.

"What time is it?" she mumbled, eyes only half open.

I picked up my cell phone from the nightstand to check. "Just after nine."

She sat straight up, taking the sheet with her. "Do you think the road is clear yet? I told Jackson I would come in early to file that police report."

That wasn't exactly the morning I had in mind.

"Probably not," I said, pulling her back to me. "I'm sure he'll understand if you're a little late. You know, the weather and all." I kissed her and ran my hands through her hair.

She melted into my arms and kissed me back. Maybe I'd get my version of a good morning after all.

BY TEN-THIRTY, we were on the road, heading not toward Rosemary Mountain, but up to Daphne's cottage instead. She wanted to change clothes, she explained, feeling embarrassed about wearing the same thing into town she had been wearing at the hospital the night before. She thought it would be a dead giveaway that she had spent the night with me.

I tried to explain to her that men rarely noticed those things, and I doubted Jackson was any different. But she reminded me that he was a detective, trained to be observant. I couldn't argue with her there, although frankly, I thought she might be exaggerating the type of training he'd had as a deputy in a small county. But she wanted to change, and I wanted to make her happy, so we battled the slick road up to her house.

I was glad to see there was no sign of fresh intrusion. I didn't like thinking that someone who'd been desperate enough to break into her place was still out there—and still likely believed Daphne had the key to the treasure.

"I'll be right back," she said, before giving me a quick kiss. "Make yourself comfortable. I'm just going to change and brush my teeth."

"Hey," I said, clearing my throat awkwardly. "While you're at it, why don't you pack a bag with whatever you need for a few days? I'd feel better if you stayed with me until they catch whoever broke into your house. Or at least find the treasure, so you're out of the spotlight."

She gave me a look that I couldn't quite read. "Well…" She bit her lip, hesitant. "Okay. Yeah, I can pack a bag for one more night. Surely they'll catch him today or tomorrow, don't you think?"

"Maybe," I said, wondering why she was so resistant to staying with me longer than that. It wasn't quite the reaction I was hoping for, but at least I knew she would be safe for another night.

She bit her lip again and nodded, then headed up the stairs, never dropping that strange look from her face.

Chapter Thirty-One

Daphne

I left Emerson downstairs so I could change and, apparently, pack an overnight bag. I was overwhelmed, to say the least.

The truth was, I had never spent the night at a man's house before. I'd liked it. A lot. I loved waking up in his arms, having our morning coffee together, and going with him to let the dog outside and the chickens out of their coop. So, part of me was thrilled he had asked me to stay again.

But the other part of me was scared that I would get too comfortable and then it would be taken away from me. Emerson was an independent man who had moved out here for solitude. He had made that clear from the beginning. I knew he was only inviting me to stay because he was a protective sort of guy who would never forgive himself if something happened to me when he could have stopped it by being there. When the case was over, he would undoubtedly want his home and privacy back.

No matter how he said he felt, I knew better than to get too attached.

I probably shouldn't have let things go so far the night before. But I couldn't really regret it. I loved him, even if that meant something different to me than it did to him. Even if it meant I wanted a future he wasn't likely to give me. Even if I knew that, inevitably, he would leave.

Everyone always leaves me.

The tears came unexpectedly. There was still a wound there, a wound from so much loss. The loss of my first mother, whose death I still didn't understand. The loss of the mother who raised me, but had walked away completely after her and Dad's divorce. The loss of my dad, the one person I'd thought would never leave.

My only serious boyfriend had also left me, after falling for another girl in college. He and I had dated for two years, had planned futures together, only for him to fall in love with someone else and leave me behind.

Emerson had already walked away once. My rational side told me things were different this time. At least, that's what I wanted to believe.

I loved Emerson, and I wanted to enjoy whatever time we had together.

But I knew the truth. The only person I could really count on was myself.

"You okay?" Emerson asked, concern on his face when I came down the stairs with my overnight bag. My face always betrayed me when I cried. A touch of makeup had done little to hide my puffy eyes.

"Yeah, I'm fine!" I said too brightly. "Let's head on to the station and get this over with."

He gave me a strange look but didn't say a word. He just took my bag and carried it to the truck while I locked up.

The sun was shining brightly, and the temperature had warmed up, mostly clearing the slush from the roads. But the snow in the woods, protected by shade, was still unspoiled.

"It's so beautiful," I said with a wistful sigh. I gazed out the window as Emerson guided the truck down the mountain. "You told me it would be, but it's even better than I imagined."

"It really is," he agreed. "It's my favorite time of year."

He reached over and took my hand, then brought it to his mouth for a kiss. "And I think I'll enjoy this winter even more than normal."

I smiled at him and tried to enjoy the moment without worrying about how things would end.

The drive to the station felt too short. Even though I needed to get the report over with, I wasn't quite ready to face the real world.

After going through Rosemary Mountain's version of security—an old metal detector I wasn't even sure was actually working—Jackson met us himself. He grinned when he saw me, but nodded curtly to Emerson. I could feel Emerson tense up beside me. The two definitely didn't like each other, but I was fairly certain Emerson was wrong about the reason. I hadn't picked up on any romantic interest from Jackson whatsoever.

Instead of taking us where he had interviewed me before, Jackson led us back to what appeared to be a breakroom. Emerson and I sat together on the couch, while Jackson pulled up a chair across from us. I had to stifle a giggle when Emerson put his arm around me, clearly wanting to indicate our relationship status.

"Alright, Daphne, let's start with the report," Jackson suggested. We got through it fairly quickly, as I didn't have much information for it.

When we finished, Emerson spoke up. "I'd like to know how far you've gotten on the investigation," he said. His voice carried the weight of authority. "Have you identified any suspects for the break-in? Do you think it's the same person who killed Wesley Adams? Have you located the unidentified man from the library yet?"

Jackson turned toward him with a cool look. "I'm afraid I can't discuss the investigation with you."

"Look," Emerson said, his voice rising. "Daphne could be in danger, and we need to know what you're doing about it."

"I understand your concern," Jackson conceded. He leaned his head back and looked up at the ceiling for a beat, then sighed.

He looked at us with something like regret on his face. "We're doing everything we can," he said in a low voice. "Unfortunately, we just don't know yet who broke into Daphne's house. There are no real leads there.

It might have been the unidentified man from the library, but we can't prove that, and we haven't located him yet. There have been a few tips as to his whereabouts, but he's managed to give us the slip every time we get close. We're still actively working that angle, though. Okay? Trust me, I'm as anxious as you are to get this case wrapped up. I'll be sure to let you both know if we make any headway on finding out who did this."

Emerson nodded, satisfied.

Jackson turned back to me. "Okay, now I'd like to talk to you about what you learned on your trip to Arkansas." He glanced Emerson's way. "Perhaps you could step out?"

Before Emerson responded, I put a hand on his knee and spoke first. "I've already told Emerson everything about that, so he might as well stay."

Jackson frowned. "Okay then. Go ahead. Just leave out any details I shouldn't know, like if you broke into any offices or anything while you were investigating." His eyes twinkled as he said the last bit.

My cheeks flushed. I had almost forgotten about that past incident. "I didn't do anything illegal, I promise. The worst I did was a little flirting to get the guy to talk."

Emerson's hand tightened on my shoulder.

Jackson chuckled. "Perfect. Well, I want to know all about that."

"Okay." I went through the whole story, yet again. Frankly, I was getting tired of the whole thing. What had initially felt like a fun adventure was no longer any fun at all. I just wanted Jackson to find the person–or persons–responsible for Wesley's death and Fiona's heart attack. And for him to somehow clear my dad's name so people would stop thinking I had any part of the treasure.

Jackson's eyes shone in appreciation as I wrapped up the story. "Fantastic," he said. "That's a whole lot more to go on than I had, as far as the treasure goes. Julie sure didn't tell me all that. I read through every page of that dang journal, and I've got to tell you, I wasn't sure why Mr. Adams would have thought it led to buried treasure. But knowing his theory will hopefully give us another lead. Speaking of which..."

He pulled the journal from his case and placed it on the table beside him.

"I'm going to finish filing this report," he said, standing. "If you two wouldn't mind waiting in here. Shouldn't be too long. But you never know. The copier acts up sometimes. Might take me half an hour or so. Maybe you can use the time to think over that conversation with Mr. Wallace again and see if you make any more connections." He winked at me and walked out, leaving the journal on the table.

CHAPTER THIRTY-TWO

Daphne

I looked at Emerson in astonishment, wondering if he interpreted what had just happened the same way I did. His face confirmed it.

"Should I?" I whispered.

He glanced around the corners of the room. "I guess so. I don't see any cameras in here, and he obviously means for you to look at it. I don't like it. But he's the one who left it here."

I nodded. It made me a little nervous to pick it up. I knew it was likely considered evidence, and therefore, it was probably against the rules for Jackson to give it to me. Now I understood why he had brought us here instead of to his desk or even to an interrogation room. He definitely wanted me to read it. I just hoped it didn't come back to bite either of us.

Emerson left me on the couch, acting as if he needed to stretch his legs. I knew he was really monitoring the hallway so that he could give me a heads up if anyone headed our way.

I picked up the journal and began flipping through it, scanning pages as quickly as I could. I wasn't sure what I was looking for, or why

Jackson wanted me to read it. But I would take any clue to the treasure I could find.

The first several pages were interesting, but didn't seem to hold any relevant information. They were about dresses she had ordered, items she needed to purchase, and some notes about a woman in town she apparently disliked.

But an entry further on caught my attention. It read:

I went to our special place today, the place no one knows about. The Kid had been there too, apparently. More was missing. He better have a nice surprise for me soon, because if it turns out he's back to his old tricks, I won't go along with his plans. Despite what some may think, I do have my pride. I decided to move it all. If he wants it back, he'll have to prove it, and he'll have to have my help getting it, as I took it to the place where men dare not go.

I got chill bumps as I read this passage, stuck in the middle of what was otherwise a rather boring diary entry. I saw what I assumed Wesley Adams had seen in it, the subtle capitalization of the word "Kid." She wasn't talking about a child taking something; she was referring to Kid Curry himself. Based on what Steve Wallace had told me, "back to his old tricks" might mean blowing money on prostitutes again. That would be enough to make any woman angry, even if that's how she had gotten involved with him.

And as for the place where men dare not go? Well, that immediately made me think of the curse.

I turned my attention back to the book, eager to read more, but my vision blurred. Before I knew what was happening, I was seeing scenes from another time and place.

A woman, furtively making her way through the woods. She held a box close to her chest with one hand, and held up her skirts in the other, carefully weaving through the brush, glancing around as if making sure no one was following her. She lifted her skirts higher to climb over a log, revealing a pistol concealed in a lace garter.

She made her way through the brush to a particularly unique tree.

Instead of growing straight, it had become deformed, growing sideways, then back up again. She walked directly below the spot where it turned back to the sky and pulled a knife from her belt. She began to dig, still looking around constantly. She wasn't nervous, not exactly, but—

"Daphne!" Emerson shook me. "Are you okay?"

It was a jarring return to reality.

"Shhh," I warned him, not wanting to attract any attention. "I'm fine."

"You didn't look fine," he said, frowning. "I thought you had passed out."

"Really, I'm alright," I said. "I'll explain everything later. Not here, okay?"

"Okay." His tone was hesitant, and concern was written on his face. I wanted to explain, but it wasn't something I wanted to get into until we were somewhere more private. This wasn't the place for another conversation about my visions, and I didn't want anyone to overhear what I had seen. I trusted Jackson, and of course, I trusted Greg, but who knew about the other people who worked there?

We heard footsteps approaching. I quickly placed the journal back on the table, right where Jackson had left it. Moments later, Jackson and Greg both walked into the room. Jackson smoothly walked over to the table, blocking the view of the journal from Greg's sight.

So I was right. He could have gotten in trouble for letting me see it.

"Hey, man," Greg said, slapping Emerson on the shoulder. "Detective Ford told me you two were here together. Nice of you to drive Daphne in so she could file that report. And Daphne, glad you're back safely from Little Rock." He grinned, looking back and forth between the two of us.

I felt like somehow he already knew we had spent the night together, and I blushed furiously. Gossip always spread like wildfire in Rosemary Mountain.

"Thanks, it's good to be back," I said, my face still burning. I stood to leave. "Was that all you needed, Detective Ford?"

Jackson nodded. "Yep. I'll follow up with you later," he said, giving me a pointed look.

Emerson frowned again and put his hand firmly on my lower back. "Should we go get some lunch?" he asked me.

"Sounds great," I answered. "Well, thanks again, Detective Ford. Sheriff Morrison."

Greg grinned and slapped Emerson on the back again. "See you two later."

We said our goodbyes and headed for the door. The whole thing felt entirely too drawn out for me. I was anxious to tell Emerson what I had seen.

I couldn't wait to tell him I knew exactly where the treasure was.

CHAPTER THIRTY-THREE

Emerson

I WAITED UNTIL WE WERE ALONE IN MY TRUCK BEFORE turning to Daphne.

"Okay, what's going on?" I asked, even though I was pretty sure I knew the answer. I had never witnessed one of her visions, but I had a feeling that's what was coming.

She took a deep breath and smoothed back her hair. "I know this is weird for you, but I, well—"

"Had a vision," I said, finishing the sentence for her.

A quick look of relief flashed across her face. "Yeah."

I nodded, trying to look reassuring. Her visions had been an awkward topic between us ever since she'd told me about them. I didn't really believe in such things, and frankly, I had wondered if she was suffering from delusions. But I trusted her now. And, truth be told, my time with Fiona was making me wonder if maybe I didn't understand everything about how the world worked after all.

"I saw where she buried it," Daphne said, whispering even though we were alone in the truck.

"The gold?"

She shook her head. "I don't think it could be gold. The box was too small, and it didn't seem to be heavy. Steve said Annie Rogers was arrested for passing banknotes associated with one of Kid Curry's robberies. I think that's what was in the box. There was a passage in her diary about moving something because the Kid was taking from it. She said she took it to the place where men dare not go."

I frowned. "The place where men dare not go? That's not very helpful."

"Emerson, think about it," Daphne said. "Remember what I told you about the curse? That's got to be it. Besides, that's where Wesley Adams was murdered."

"That makes sense." I mulled it over, scratching my beard. "But unless you saw something more specific than that, it might take us a long time to find it. That area up there is huge, and mostly overgrown at this point. It could be anywhere. If it were gold coins, we could get a metal detector to help, but if it's banknotes..."

"I did see," she said, her face shining with excitement. "There was a tree. It was very unique. It didn't grow straight up. The trunk turned sideways and then back up again at a ninety-degree angle. Like an arm that someone was holding up with a bent elbow."

My jaw dropped. I knew exactly what tree she was talking about.

I grabbed my phone and did a quick search. "Is this it?" I asked, showing her the picture.

"Yes! Exactly!" She practically squealed with excitement.

"It's called a signal tree. Indigenous Americans who lived throughout this region would bend young saplings to make them grow that way, using them as trail markers," I explained. "Once bent, the trees would continue growing in that direction forever. Many of them are gone now, but there are a few remaining ones—including one at the top of that trail."

"We have to go there," she said. "That's where it is. Emerson, we can find it!"

"It's too bad it snowed last night," I commented. "It'll melt quickly here in town, but up there on the mountain with the shade of the trees, the trail could be covered in snow for a few days."

She sat back, momentarily deflated. Then a grin crept across her face. "Hey, remember our first date?"

"Of course." I smiled. I would never forget that first date with her.

"Remember how you told me you love to snowshoe and that you would teach me someday? I think today's the day." She grinned at me, and my heart filled with warmth like I had never felt before.

I couldn't help myself. I leaned over and kissed her softly, right there in the parking lot, wishing there was privacy for so much more. Since there wasn't, I reluctantly broke the kiss and settled for putting my hand on her thigh.

"As much as I would love to teach you, I'm afraid we don't have enough snow for that," I said gently. "You need a minimum of eight inches of fluffy snow like this, or you'll damage your snowshoes. A foot of snow is better. We only got three inches last night. Enough to mess up the mountain roads, but not enough to snowshoe, I'm afraid."

"Hmm." She sat back, contemplating again. "How tough would it be to just walk up the trail with three inches of snow?"

I moved my head from side to side, contemplating it. "It's definitely doable," I said. "And maybe even a little easier in some ways, if the snow smooths out the path on those rocky sections. But we'll have to go slow. Some of those areas are a little steep, and the snow will make it slippery."

Truth be told, I knew I could make it up easily. Three inches of snow wasn't that big of a deal, and the trail wasn't that difficult. But I had never hiked with Daphne before, and I wasn't sure what her endurance was even in ideal conditions.

She nodded, her face serious. "Let's do it. The quicker we get up there, the quicker we can find out if the treasure is still there. If it is, I can clear my dad's name."

"And take the spotlight off of you," I pointed out. "You're right. We need to get up there. Do you have snow boots?"

She laughed. "Yes, but not the kind you're thinking of. Is there a store around here where I can pick up some real ones?"

I started the truck. "Yep. There's an outfitter store up the road. They'll get you hooked up. I have some extra poles you can use to help in any slippery spots. Let's get you some boots and grab an early lunch at Marco's. We should be able to hit the trail by two at the latest. If we give ourselves an hour to get up and an hour back down, we'll have a solid hour to look for the treasure before we risk losing light."

She nodded gravely and squeezed my hand before turning her head to gaze out the window.

Somehow, I felt I knew exactly what she was thinking. The idea of finding the treasure was exciting, for sure. But if the area hadn't been recently disturbed and the treasure was missing? That would open up a whole new can of worms for her.

We needed the treasure to be there.

Chapter Thirty-Four

Daphne

A couple of hours later, I found myself back in the parking lot of the trailhead where this whole thing had started. Oh, how things had changed, and in such a short time.

The mood of the mountain was completely different in the snow. It felt peaceful, serene. Or maybe I was projecting my own mood onto it. Despite everything that had gone wrong, one thing had finally gone right. And I was determined to enjoy every minute with Emerson, instead of dwelling on the inevitable end.

I felt like a real mountaineer, bundled up in new snow pants and snow boots and carrying Emerson's hiking poles. He showed me how the attached "baskets" would prevent them from going deep into the snow if we ever got enough to actually have our snowshoeing adventure. I enjoyed hearing him talk about the future, even if I knew not to hope for one.

"You ready?" Emerson asked, adding a few last-minute things to his pack before swinging it onto his back.

"Yep." I grinned. I was more than ready. I couldn't wait to get to the top to see if the treasure was still there.

"Let's do this. But listen, stay close, okay?" He said the words quietly, with a smile on his face that didn't match his tone.

My body immediately went on alert. "The bears will be in hibernation by now, right?"

He pulled me close to him and snuggled in, creating the picture of two people out for a romantic date. "I'm not talking about bears," he said, whispering in my ear. "We aren't the first ones here."

"What do you mean?" I whispered back, confused. We were clearly the only vehicle at the trailhead.

"There are boot tracks at the start of the trail. Someone's been here, and they came on foot." He kept snuggling me and smiling, stopping to kiss me before bending back down to my ear. "Could be nothing. Could be a backpacker hiking through the hills here. But considering the situation..."

I let out a breath. "Got it. Okay, I'll stay close."

He kissed me one more time. "That's my girl."

My heart felt like it might burst.

He broke away and headed toward the trailhead. I followed close behind, finally seeing what he had spotted so quickly. Tracks cut across the edge of the parking lot and headed straight up the trail. My belly cramped with fear. Yes, it was likely just a backpacker. And if not, odds were it was just a treasure hunter and not the killer. But it still made me nervous.

We hiked quietly at first, Emerson apparently on high alert, watching for whoever had made the tracks. But after a while, he relaxed a bit and broke the silence.

"Aren't the woods beautiful in the snow?"

I looked around, taking in the scene. "They really are," I agreed. "Everything seems so magical, so fresh."

"Exactly. I love it. It brings back so many fun memories of being a kid. Having snowball fights with my brothers, building snow forts, racing across the fields in snowmobiles. I love it here, but I gotta admit, I miss Wisconsin winters. We only get a little taste of it here."

"Do you think you'll ever move back?" I asked, regretting the words even as they left my lips. I knew as soon as I asked them that I was afraid of the answer.

He paused a beat before answering. "I don't know," he said. "Before, I would have said no. It was just too hard being there. Too many memories. And Ken's girl, Sarah, still lives there in town. I feel so much guilt every time I see her. Felt easier to live far away without those constant reminders. But now that things have changed? Maybe. I miss my family, and I really love it there."

My heart sank, even though it was the answer I expected. He had only moved here to get space from Ken's death, and now that he was healing, it made sense he would go home. I had always felt how deeply he loved it there.

But the thought of him leaving Rosemary Mountain made my heart ache. It hurt so much that I couldn't seem to hold to my resolution of just enjoying the time we had.

"You're awfully quiet," he commented a few minutes later.

"Am I? Sorry. I guess the trail's getting harder," I said, trying to make an excuse.

"Do you need a break?" He glanced back to check on me, making my heart swell again.

"No, it's okay. Let's keep pushing."

"Okay. But tell me if you need to stop for a minute. I've got water in my pack."

"I'm good right now, but thanks." I managed a smile, and he turned back to the trail, seemingly satisfied.

BEFORE LONG, the heaviness in my heart began to lift. I didn't talk much on the trail—I was too out of breath. But Emerson kept me entertained, telling me stories about growing up with his brothers. It seemed to do him good to talk about it, and despite how much I longed for him to stay in Rosemary Mountain, I enjoyed the stories and was laughing out loud before long. Having grown up without siblings, their shenanigans were completely foreign to me. It was clear Emerson's childhood had been full of love and laughter, two things that had been in short supply during my own.

But as we neared the end of the trail, Emerson grew quiet as well.

When the clearing was in sight, he stopped in his tracks. I caught up with him and hugged him from behind.

"Thank you for telling me those stories," I said.

He turned back to me with a warning in his eyes and held a finger to his lips. "Stay at least six feet back. Preferably off to the side, behind a tree. I need to scope things out before we move forward," he whispered, drawing the pistol he always carried from his back. He gestured to the mystery boot tracks we had been following.

I nodded and moved back, fear gripping me again.

He moved forward slowly, listening closely for any sounds. He held the gun discreetly down at his side and watched for several minutes before finally stepping into the clearing.

I could tell it was empty by the way his shoulders dropped.

"What now?" I whispered.

He gestured for me to come to his side, where he could whisper into my ear.

"The tree you saw is that way," he said, pointing ahead to the right. "But these tracks are heading somewhere different." He pointed to the left. "The official trail continues straight ahead, so the backpacker theory is looking less likely. We have a choice to make. We can go to the tree as planned. But whoever is out here might follow our tracks there. Or we can follow these tracks and try to find the guy."

"Deliberately try to find the guy who might have killed Wesley?" My whisper came out in a squeak.

"Better to know where your enemy is."

"Okay. I trust you," I said, looking up into his eyes.

He gave me a look that let me know those words meant the world to him before nodding and warning me to be as quiet as possible.

Then he started following the tracks.

CHAPTER THIRTY-FIVE

Daphne

BEING AS QUIET AS POSSIBLE WAS HARDER THAN I EXPECTED in snow pants. With every step, the thick pants brushed against each other, making a swishing sound. Still, I tried, even adjusting my stride to an awkward wide-legged walk, trying to keep the fabric quiet.

Emerson's wool hiking pants didn't have the same problem. He moved gracefully through the woods without making a sound. He had told me his military experience was medical, but I found myself wondering if he had other training he hadn't shared with me. He moved with ease and seemed to know exactly what he was doing as he tracked the mystery hiker.

After a few minutes, he stopped and crouched, gesturing for me to come closer.

"Look," he said. "He was digging."

Sure enough, there was a fresh dig site beside a large boulder. Whoever had dug there had done a thorough job, probably assuming the boulder was a site marker.

"Do you think he found anything?" I whispered. I had confidence in my vision, but it was possible the treasure had been moved at some point.

Emerson pointed at the boot prints in the snow. "The tracks keep going, so I doubt it. If he found something here, he probably would have headed back down the mountain."

I looked around Emerson and saw where he was pointing. He was right—the tracks continued on through the woods, veering to the right this time.

"So we keep going?"

He nodded. "We keep going."

WE FOLLOWED THE TRACKS FARTHER, and soon came to yet another dig site. This one was beside another unique tree. It wasn't the trail tree from my vision, but it had what appeared to be an old scar from a lightning strike. The man we were following had dug all around it, too. Again, the tracks continued, giving us hope that he still hadn't found it.

But as we followed the tracks, Emerson stopped suddenly and frowned, then pulled out his compass.

"What is it?" I asked.

"We're heading back to the clearing," he said in a low tone. "I don't like that. Stay close."

I nodded and followed behind him again, still trying to be as quiet as possible. Soon, it was clear Emerson was right about his bearings. The trees thinned, and we came to the edge of the clearing from a different spot in the tree line. Emerson approached slowly, still holding his gun, careful to maintain cover as long as possible. He got to the edge and scanned the area, then dropped his shoulders. I wasn't sure if it was relief or disappointment.

"He's gone," he said flatly.

I came up beside him, and he showed me what he saw. The tracks went straight through the clearing and back down the trail—tracks that hadn't been there when we first arrived.

"So he was here, probably digging, when we arrived," I said.

"Yeah. Maybe he heard us following him, and that's why he left."

I nodded. "Maybe."

Or maybe he had found the treasure.

Emerson pulled out his cell phone and took pictures of the clearest boot prints. "For Greg," he explained.

"You mean Jackson," I corrected him, an amused grin on my face. He rolled his eyes. I didn't mind. I thought his jealousy was a little cute, even though there was absolutely no reason for it.

When he finished snapping photographs, he checked his watch. "We made decent time up the trail. If you're up to it, we still have time to check our original location. We might walk the last fifteen minutes back in the dark, but I have flashlights."

The thought of walking that trail in the dark, even with flashlights, chilled me to the bone. But we were already here, and it was clear someone else was still searching. There really wasn't any other option. We needed to get to the trail tree as quickly as possible.

"Let's do it," I said with a shrug, trying to act braver than I felt.

He gave me a grin, then led the way, cutting across the clearing to the tree line on the other side.

"How do you know where we're going?" I asked.

"There's an old trail here," he explained. "It's not the official one that gets maintained regularly by the county. It's a shame, really. The signal tree is such a special thing, you'd think they would build a walking trail around it. But they have limited resources, and they focus on the other trail. If you keep going up that one, it leads to a pretty cool natural spring and waterfall, and it's easier terrain. They see it as more of a tourist draw, I guess. But there are a few of us who like to get off that main trail, so this one gets cut back a few times a year by those of us who like to hike it."

"That's awesome that you guys take care of it. But I'm guessing that means the trail tree isn't much of a secret then, huh?"

"Definitely not a secret. It's still a landmark around here."

"I wonder why our mystery treasure hunter didn't go there today," I mused.

"That's a good question."

We fell into silence as he led me up a trail that only he recognized. I felt like we were walking through uncharted woods, and could only trust that he knew where we were going. But after a while, I noticed an occasional swipe of white paint along a tree. The paint swatches were subtle and faded, but they were there. This was a trail after all, albeit a difficult one to follow if you didn't know what you were looking for.

The terrain grew more difficult, with some fairly steep patches. More than once, Emerson had to grab my hand and help me up the slippery, snow-covered rocks. But after a bit, it leveled out again, and when the trail tree came into view, it was all worth it.

I breathed out a long breath and shook my head in disbelief. "It's really here. I know my visions are real, but it still always blows my mind to see the evidence. And how amazing to see and touch a piece of history." I circled the tree, tracing it with my hand, in awe of what it was and the role it had played.

"It's pretty awesome," Emerson agreed. He lowered his pack and pulled a small shovel from it. "Now tell me where to dig."

I looked at the shovel and laughed. "I feel so silly. I didn't even think about us needing a shovel. But you seem to have everything in your pack."

"Well, this is kind of an important tool to carry if you're backpacking."

"A shovel? Really? Why?"

He looked at me as if unsure whether I was pulling his leg. "You know. For cat holes."

"Cat holes? What are you talking about?" I was utterly confused.

He ran a hand over his face and chuckled. "For burying human feces when you're backpacking."

"Oh. I see. Well. Yes, I guess that is an important tool to have." I laughed once, then couldn't stop giggling.

Emerson shook his head, an amused look on his face. "And just what is so funny?"

"This," I said, gesturing around us. "You can't imagine how boring my life used to be. But we just tracked a potential murderer through the woods. Now, we're going to use a poop shovel to dig for buried treasure." The laughter started again, this time so hard I had tears in my eyes. "It's just hilarious. My life has become stranger than I ever imagined possible."

Emerson started laughing too, a deep laugh that seemed to fill the woods. By the time we both stopped, it was clear we both felt lighter, happier, and better for it. The tension from tracking the hiker was gone, and my worries about Emerson moving home were shelved for another day. For now—in this moment at least—we were just Daphne and Emerson, having fun on an adventure together.

"So where should I dig?" he asked again.

"In my vision, it was right below the bend," I said, walking to the elbow and pointing down. "But that was over a hundred years ago. So I'm guessing a little farther in than that, to account for the growth."

"Got it." He walked over to the tree and squatted down, using the shovel to remove the snow from the ground. I propped myself on a tree stump and watched, wanting to help but not sure how without a second shovel.

After a few minutes, he frowned again. "Come look at this," he said.

I walked over to where he was digging. "What is it?" I asked.

"I think someone already dug here."

I looked closer, but didn't see whatever he did. "Help me out. What makes you think that?"

"Well, for one thing, there are no dead leaves under here." He moved away from the tree and quickly shoveled snow off another spot. "See? It's still early in the season. The leaves haven't decomposed yet. But there aren't any here, like someone raked them away. And look at this." He walked back underneath the tree and squatted down, using the shovel to loosen a spot. "See that?"

I looked closely. "It's grass, but it's upside down."

"Exactly. Someone dug here and replaced the dirt. But they didn't bother to turn the soil the right way up."

"Oh, no." My heart sank. "So someone beat us to it."

He nodded. "We should still dig, in case they missed it. But I'm afraid so."

With that, all the joy of the search was gone. My only real lead to the treasure was a dead end. Emerson continued to dig, but my hopes were dashed. And frankly, I was more concerned than ever that Dad had found the treasure. After all, if the killer had found it here, why would he still be digging?

Of course, we didn't have proof that the man we were following today was actually the killer, or any real reason to think so, honestly, other than just pure hope that we were getting close to finding him. Half the town was probably searching for the treasure in their off time.

So, I reminded myself, even if it wasn't here, that didn't mean my dad was guilty of taking it.

It just meant I didn't yet have a way of proving his innocence.

AFTER A FEW MINUTES, Emerson called me over again. "Look at this," he said.

I hopped off my stump and ran over. He placed an earring in my hand.

"Do you think it's part of the treasure?" he asked in a hopeful tone.

It was a fairly large pearl, surrounded by gemstones in a flower shape. I examined it closely.

"No, I don't," I said, disappointed. "I'm not a jewelry expert by any means, and I don't really know what jewelry was like in nineteen hundred. But this looks like something from the fifties or sixties to me. It reminds me of something from the glamorous movies made then. You know, Audrey Hepburn and Marilyn Monroe type stuff. I was obsessed with those movies as a kid, and used to buy costume pieces from yard sales. Also," I said, pausing to rub the pearl against my teeth, "it's fake."

"Damn," he said, letting out a breath. "I was hoping we had something."

I frowned. "We might, actually."

"How's that?"

"I don't know. But I feel like I've seen this before." I closed my eyes, trying to remember. My eyes popped back open. "Oh, my goodness. Was Julie wearing these?"

"Who's Julie?" he asked, his face blank.

"Wesley's girlfriend. Remember?"

Recognition dawned on his face. "Oh, yeah, I completely forgot her name. I don't know if she was wearing them. I really didn't pay attention. I was only looking at you that day."

My heart melted, and I smiled despite the situation. I looked down at the earring again. "I know I've seen these before. I think she was wearing them that day. And it makes sense." I smacked my forehead. "Her boyfriend was a historian who frequented estate sales. Of course, he would buy her vintage jewelry."

"If she was wearing them that day, that means—"

"It means instead of going home when they released her, she kept searching for the treasure."

Our eyes met, both realizing the implication.

"We've got to tell Jackson," I said.

Emerson sighed and started putting things back in his pack.

"Alright. Let's go."

CHAPTER THIRTY-SIX

Emerson

WE PACKED UP AND HEADED BACK DOWN THE TRAIL. I TRIED
to keep my demeanor as relaxed as possible for Daphne's sake, but the
truth was, I had a bad feeling about whoever had been up on that
mountain with us. I kept a close eye out as we hiked back down,
knowing how easy it would be for someone to make boot tracks down
the trail, then double back and hide in the woods, waiting for us. I
would never forgive myself if Daphne got hurt again on my watch.

I didn't breathe easy until we were back in my truck.

Daphne insisted on calling Jackson, not Greg. I knew she was right,
but I didn't like that either. Despite knowing that nothing ever
happened between her and Jackson, I still didn't totally trust him. I
wasn't sure why, but something about his vibe felt off to me. Maybe it
was my loyalty to Greg. Maybe it was my concern for Daphne's safety.
Either way, I didn't like how Jackson kept letting Daphne get involved
in the investigation. It wasn't right.

Although it might not be fair to judge him for that, considering
how I had just taken Daphne on a hunt for a potential killer through the
forest.

Whether I liked it or not, Daphne just had a way of getting involved in things.

SHE HUNG up the phone and told me to head back to my place. "Jackson's going to meet us there," she said. "He's already in the area and said he could be there in ten minutes. He wants the pictures you took and the earring. He said he doesn't remember if Julie was wearing the earrings at the station, but he has security camera footage, so he can check."

"Either way, they're likely hers," I pointed out. "Even if she wasn't wearing them then. Like you said, it makes sense that Wes would have bought her antique jewelry."

"That's true. But I do feel like I've seen them before, so I'd like the confirmation that she was wearing them. Although..." She trailed off and sighed.

"Although what?"

"I don't know. Julie was so sad and scared that day. She's very young." Daphne got quiet and looked out the window before continuing. "Like I told you before, I collected a lot of things like this as a kid. Maybe I'm just thinking I recognize them because they look so similar to ones I used to own. I hate to get Julie in trouble."

I leaned over and patted her hand before putting the truck into reverse. "I think you just have a soft spot for young girls. First Christie, now Julie. You're protective of them."

She smiled ruefully. "Maybe so."

"But if she was involved, she has to answer for it," I reminded her. "I'm sure Greg and Jackson will figure out the truth."

"You're right. I just feel guilty."

"Don't feel guilty. You're not the one who murdered the guy."

WE GOT BACK to my cabin and shed our hiking gear just in time to answer the door for Jackson. He greeted Daphne with his normal stupid grin, but I managed to refrain from rolling my eyes.

I texted him the pictures I had taken of the boot prints and told him the whole story about tracking the guy and the dig sites. Then Daphne pulled out the earring and gave it to him. He used a handkerchief to take it from her and quickly dropped it into a plastic bag before examining it.

"Hmm..." He frowned. "On my way over here, I put in a call for one of the deputies to check the security footage for sure. But I'm thinking you may be right, Daphne. These really might be Julie's. Which doesn't necessarily mean she killed Wes. She could just be searching for the treasure. But I'm kicking myself for letting her go so quickly."

"She seemed so innocent," Daphne said, reassuring him. "Maybe she is."

"You know what bothers me? She never told us about the man Wesley was with at the library. The one who keeps slipping through our fingers." Jackson frowned again and pursed his lips. "Which makes me wonder if they're in it together."

Daphne looked shocked, but then seemed to consider it. "I don't know. Maybe. She really seemed to love Wesley. At least she acted that way. But, at the same time, she ran away when she found out he had been murdered. I just don't know."

"I don't either," Jackson said gravely. "But you can bet I'm going to find out if she really went home to Little Rock, like she said. And if not, she's going to have a lot of explaining to do."

I sat quietly, listening to their conversation, but I had questions of my own. And I wanted answers.

"How on earth does this man keep slipping through your fingers? Are you even trying?" I asked, my tone flat.

Jackson's nostrils flared as he stared me down. "Of course I'm trying. We all are. But he's apparently hiding in the woods, and in case you haven't noticed, we have a heck of a lot of wilderness to cover here. That's actually why I was so close by when Daphne called," he said, nodding her way. "Someone called in earlier and said they saw someone with a similar description camping illegally here on the mountain last night. We went out to check the area, but the guy had already moved on. There was definite evidence of someone having camped there, though."

I nodded. "Based on the size of the boot prints we were tracking, I'm guessing they belonged to a man with size eleven feet. Does that match up with the man you're looking for?"

Jackson shrugged. "Obviously, Emerson, I haven't seen his feet. But I'd say it's possible it was the same guy."

"We have to find him. And Julie." Daphne's voice was determined.

"The sheriff's office will handle that," Jackson said pointedly. It was a mark in his favor as far as I was concerned. I wanted to help Daphne find the treasure, but today's experience had brought it back home how dangerous this situation really was. There was a killer out there searching for the treasure, too.

The last thing I wanted was for Daphne to go after him. Or her.

CHAPTER THIRTY-SEVEN

Daphne

FOR THE SECOND MORNING IN A ROW, I WOKE IN EMERSON'S arms. It was still so surreal. I felt happier and more loved than I could ever remember having felt. I stayed still, not wanting to wake him, simply wanting to enjoy every moment of lying there curled up on his chest.

But just as I relaxed enough to nearly doze off again, his alarm went off. He slapped it with a groan.

"Ugh." He ran a hand over his face. "I'm supposed to work today." He rolled over so he was facing me and kissed me on the forehead. "But I could call in."

"Don't be silly." I tucked my head underneath his chin and snuggled in close, enjoying the feeling of his strong arms wrapped around me. "You have to work, and I do, too," I said, feeling a stab of guilt for how little time I had invested in rebuilding my business. I had some work I could do, yes, but not enough. And it was entirely my fault. Had my focus been on my business, I could have gotten some additional clients by now.

Emerson sighed. "I don't feel good about you going back home. Not until they catch this guy."

"I doubt he tries to break into my house during broad daylight. And we don't even know that he'll try again anyway," I pointed out. "He may have realized I didn't have anything the last time he was there."

"I don't think so. I'm thinking the reason he stopped digging yesterday and made a beeline back down the mountain was because he realized we were following him. If he knows we were up on the mountain, he'll know we know something. And since most people don't know about your visions—"

"He'll think it's because I have the journal or something else," I finished. "I see your point. I can avoid my house today, it's no problem. I was planning to visit Fiona anyway, and I need to run some errands in town. I can meet you back here tonight when you get off work."

He sighed again and pulled me even closer. "That's the thing. It's a twenty-four-hour shift. I won't be back until tomorrow."

"Oh." I should have known that. He had told me how his job worked once, but I hadn't really thought about it. I suddenly felt deflated, knowing I would go to bed alone that night and wake up without him tomorrow morning.

I knew in that moment that I wanted to wake up with him every morning for the rest of my life. So much for all my promises to myself to just enjoy what we had while it lasted and not worry about the fact that he probably wouldn't ever offer me a future.

"I can call in," he repeated.

"No. Don't do that." I stifled a sigh and tried to sound more certain than I felt. "You already took a full month off for your trip to Wisconsin. I'm sure you're out of PTO, and it will put them in a bind if you call in at the last minute. I'll be fine. It sounds like Jackson's getting closer to finding this guy. It may all be wrapped up before the end of the day."

"Why don't you stay here anyway?" he suggested. "I normally take Thor with me to the base, but he could stay with you. He may be old, but he's still an excellent guard dog. A German Shepherd is always a deterrent, and he's got a protective nature. I'd feel better knowing you were here, with him, than at your house alone."

My heart melted at the thought that he trusted me enough to let me stay at his house and take care of his dog.

I was falling in love with him more every day, which made the thought of losing him even more painful.

"Please," he said, when I didn't answer right away. "To make me feel better. Say you'll stay here tonight, with Thor. I know you think it's silly, and you're probably dying to get back to your own place. But this man is still out there, and if anything happened to you..."

"Alright," I agreed, leaning up to kiss him. "I'll stay here tonight. And thank you for wanting to make sure I'm safe. I do need to visit Fiona today, though."

He grinned. "I figure Fiona can keep both of you safe."

I laughed. "Yeah, I think she can."

A FEW HOURS LATER, I found myself alone at Emerson's house. It felt strangely intimate. It was an odd thing, really, that just staying alone at his house felt that way, considering how intimate things had gotten while we had stayed there together. But this was a different feeling. I liked it, even though there was a part of me that wanted to break everything off now, just to avoid how badly it would hurt when he ended things down the road.

With every day that passed like this, I felt our lives becoming more connected and myself becoming more attached. It felt like I had more to lose. When he walked away the first time, I had only lost him. It had hurt like crazy, and at that point, we had only been casually dating.

Now, I loved him. I loved him in a way I had never loved before. I was also now attached to his dog, his chickens, and even his cabin. Despite knowing better, I was imagining a future with him—marriage, kids, growing old together on the mountain.

If last time had hurt, next time would destroy me.

I was getting depressed just thinking about it. I needed to shake it off, get out of my own head, and go talk to Fiona. She always had the perspective I needed.

. . .

EMERSON HAD TAKEN me to get my car that morning, so I drove to Fiona's house. I would have preferred walking. The sun was shining, and it was a beautiful day. But I knew, even though he hadn't said it, that he didn't really want me walking alone on the mountain while this guy was still out there. So, I decided to humor him. I had to admit, I enjoyed his protectiveness.

When I pulled into Fiona's driveway, I was cheered by the sight of smoke coming from her chimney. Her house would be cozy, and if she were feeling better, she would likely have some funny stories for me. I really missed her and couldn't wait to see her.

She threw the door open before I even made it out of my car.

"Daphne!" she called out as I walked up the stone pathway. "I'm so glad you came. I was starting to think I had scared you off with my bad mood the other day."

"Never," I said, leaning in to give her a quick kiss on the cheek. She beamed and pulled me inside.

"I've got hot coffee and cinnamon rolls fresh out of the oven," she said. "Come have a seat, and we'll enjoy our little treat. I want to hear all about how you've been." Her smile changed to a sly one. "I can see you finally took my advice and had that roll in the hay with Emerson. I want to hear all about it."

"Fiona!" My jaw dropped. "How can you tell?"

She cackled. "Women always know. Come on now, how did it happen?"

I sat down at her kitchen table, debating how to answer, as she moved about the kitchen. She placed a steaming cup of coffee and the most incredible-looking cinnamon roll I had ever seen in front of me. I took a giant bite and groaned in pleasure. It was as delicious as it looked. Fiona was pure magic in the kitchen.

She sat down across from me with her own plate and scowled. "I should have kept that from you until you answered my question."

I swallowed my bite and laughed. "Sorry. I don't kiss and tell."

"Now, Daphne Sullivan, don't you do that to me. I'm nearly as invested in this relationship as you are, you know. It *is* a relationship now, isn't it? Not just you two deciding to be what the kids call 'friends with benefits,' I hope," she said with a disgusted look on her face.

I smiled. "It's a relationship." I paused for a moment, looking down at my cinnamon roll. "He says he loves me."

"Well, that's been clear as day since he met you," she said. "But what about his brother?"

I started at the beginning and told her the story of his sign from Ken, knowing that Emerson would have told her himself if he were here. After all, he had opened up to her about Ken in the first place, before even telling me about the whole thing.

By the time I was finished, she was wiping tears from her eyes. "Glory be," she said. "I'm so happy that boy's found some peace. And especially grateful he's given himself the freedom to be happy with you. But"—she peered at me closely—"why am I sensing you may not be giving yourself the same freedom?"

"I am. Happy, I mean. I love him too, and I've told him that. It's just..." I trailed off, toying with her lace tablecloth.

"It's just what?"

"I don't know. It's hard to explain. When he walked away the first time, it hurt so much. It was ridiculous how much, really, when we had only been on a few dates. It hurt more than it should have—way more than any other past breakup."

"It's different with you two," she agreed. "You're meant to be together, and I think you've both felt that since the day you met."

I couldn't disagree with her. "Maybe you're right. But the fact is, he's walked away twice now. As happy as I am with him, I find myself dreading how much it's going to hurt the next time he does it."

"Who says there's going to be a next time?"

I held my coffee mug in both hands and let out a breath. "Everybody leaves at some point, Fiona."

"Ah. I see. You mean everyone leaves *you* at some point." She pulled off a piece of her cinnamon roll and nibbled on it, deep in thought, before speaking again. "You know, if there's one thing I've learned as a midwife, it's how important the bond between mother and child is. It's sacred. And when that bond gets severed by separation, whether it be adoption or death or something else, well, it leaves a wound in the child's heart. You were a wee thing when your mama died."

Tears pricked her eyes. "Well, it was a trauma for sure, losing her like that, and so young. And then Lonnie whisked you away from here, away from everything and everyone you'd ever known, hoping you'd forget. But even if you forgot with your mind, your heart remembered. You see?"

I nodded slowly.

"Your heart remembered her. Your heart remembered *me*. Your heart even remembered that cottage. And losing so much, so young, well, of course it's hard for you to believe that anyone's really going to be here to stay. Loss has been imprinted on your heart from the beginning."

"Yeah," I said, suddenly struggling to speak past the lump in my throat. I swallowed it down with a sip of coffee, then opened up again. "That was a loss. A loss I still don't even know how to grieve. But then Mom—Janet—left me too. I know now it wasn't totally her choice, but growing up, I believed it was."

Fiona nodded. "That's a hard burden for a child to bear, believing their mother could just walk away from them."

"Yeah. I guess... I guess I've always felt like Dad was the only one who loved me. Like I wasn't really good enough to be loved for just me, but that somehow he looked past it. Then he died, and I guess I felt like I would never really be loved again."

The pain was raw now, and I couldn't stop the tears from coming. "I've dated before, but I've never truly gotten serious with anyone. I never let them in the way I let Emerson in. I've always kept a wall up, kept some emotional distance. Kept the ending in sight. But now... Fiona, I love him. And I can't keep him out. My walls break down every time he's around. I respond to him so differently than I've ever responded to anyone, like I can't help but give my heart to him. But I just know that, like everyone else, he'll leave too."

"And maybe he will," Fiona said gently. "But I don't think so. That boy has a faithful, good heart. I can see it. If he told you he loves you, you can hold on to that. And if I'm wrong and he does walk away? I'll be here, and we'll get through it. Because I can tell you this for sure. It may not mean as much, but old Fiona will never walk away from you or stop loving you. You've got me until the day I die, and even then I'll be watching over you from above." She squeezed my hand.

It meant everything.

AFTER OUR HEART-TO-HEART, Fiona asked me to catch her up on the case. I was glad to fill her in, knowing she had missed out on so much of it since her heart attack. But when I got to the part about finding the earring, she frowned.

"Describe that earring again," she said.

I did, confused by her reaction.

She got up and went to one of her bookshelves, removing a small framed picture of her from her younger days.

"Is this the earring you found?" she asked, handing me the photograph.

I was astonished. "Yes. Yes, it is. I knew I had seen it somewhere! But I don't understand. What was your earring doing there? Did you dig there at some point, for herbs or something?"

"No, I did not," she said with a grim face. "But I have an idea. I need to go into town. Do you want to come with me, dear?"

CHAPTER THIRTY-EIGHT

Daphne

As we drove down the mountain, bouncing along in Fiona's antique truck, she explained what she was thinking.

"I used to own those earrings, years and years ago," she said. "I loved them. Had bought them from a vintage shop as a kind of splurge when I had established myself enough to have some extra spending money."

"What happened to them? Did you sell them at a yard sale or something?"

"No." She shook her head. "I've made some stupid mistakes in my life, Daphne. I'll be the first to admit that. But this one is particularly embarrassing. I fell in love with the wrong man."

I couldn't help but crack a smile. "What's so embarrassing about that?"

"I should have known better. I *did* know better," she said, correcting herself. "I'm generally a pretty good judge of character, and I knew he was lacking in integrity. But, well, I'll be honest with you, Daphne." Her voice became solemn. "I've never seen a man look quite as good in a pair of jeans as he did, if you know what I mean."

I bit my lips to keep from laughing. "I see."

"His name was Phillip. He was tall and gorgeous, and he knew how to kiss you so your knees would go weak. Oh, Daphne. We did have us some fun."

"Go on," I said, still fighting back a laugh.

"Well, I told you, he was lacking integrity. And I may enjoy some fun now and again, but I've always been strictly a one-man woman, and I expect the same in return. I made that clear to him from the beginning. But, well, in case you haven't noticed, there's a decided lack of gorgeous men in this town."

"I've noticed," I said, trying to match her serious tone. "That's why Emerson gets so much attention when we go out."

"Exactly." She nodded. "And, well, Iris decided she wanted to have some fun too."

"Iris the librarian?"

"One and the same."

I had a sinking feeling about where this was going.

Fiona's voice grew angry. "She decided she was going to seduce him away from me, and oh, did she ever! This was back in the day, and I'll admit, she was a bit of a looker. Plus, she had that uptight librarian thing going on, always wearing heels, hose, and skin-tight pencil skirts. Apparently, *some* men are into that kind of thing."

"Yes," I said, once again fighting back a laugh. "I've heard that's a thing."

"Yes, well." She sniffed. "He snuck around with her for a while. He was a good liar. Oh, I knew in my gut something was wrong. But Daphne, the man was just so *talented* I couldn't help but overlook it. He could do this one thing where—"

"You know, I think we should just get back to the earring part of the story," I suggested. While I found this part of Fiona's life fascinating, I really didn't need a mental picture of her escapades.

"Alright, alright," she said, waving her hand. "One day, I went to the library to check out a book. There was Iris, looking all smug and wearing *my* earrings. That scumbag didn't have enough money to buy her anything nice himself, so he stole my earrings and gave them to *her*. I went home, confronted him, kicked him out, and I've pretty much hated her ever since."

"I'm really sorry, Fiona. That's terrible."

She waved it off. "Losing him wasn't much of a loss. Not really. I mean, I did miss the fun. But I knew all along he didn't have long-term potential. Those earrings though... That hurt."

"You think Iris was the one digging there?" I asked, my voice doubtful. "I know you're in amazing shape, Fiona, but most women your age probably wouldn't be able to go up that trail, much less dig a hole there."

"Maybe most women where you're from, but you seem to forget this is a mountain town. Women here have always had to do more to survive. Don't let Iris fool you. She's as scrappy as they come."

"Maybe you're right. But isn't it possible she sold those earrings and someone else was digging there?"

"Of course it's possible. That's why we're going to see her ourselves, instead of going straight to the sheriff. Although, can you imagine how much fun it would be to show up at the library with Sheriff Morrison? I can just picture him arresting her, right in front of all her patrons." Fiona was practically gloating.

"Now, now. Let's not get so caught up in a revenge plot that we embarrass ourselves by being wrong," I said gently. "I've done that before, remember?"

"I know, I know. But my, won't it be fun if she really did do it?"

FIONA WAS GRINNING from ear to ear when we reached the library. I could tell how badly she wanted Iris to be the murderer, but I didn't buy it. Fiona might be strong enough to kill a man with blunt force, but no matter how scrappy Iris had been in the past, I couldn't believe the prim and proper librarian I had met was strong enough to do that.

Still, for Fiona's sake, part of me hoped she was right.

Fiona marched triumphantly into the library, then immediately deflated when Iris wasn't anywhere to be seen.

Jasper, the younger librarian from before, lit up when he saw us. "Ladies," he said, making his little bow again. "What a pleasure it is to have you back in our library. How can I assist you today?"

"We're here for Iris," Fiona announced. "I have a bone to pick with her, and I need to talk to her right away."

He hesitated. "I'm so sorry. I'm afraid it's just me here today. Are you sure there's nothing I can help you with?"

"Where's Iris?" I asked.

He glanced around to make sure no one was listening, then lifted his shoulders in a quick shrug. "She called in sick four days ago. It's not like her at all. I called and checked on her the next day, but she yelled at me to leave her alone, said that she would be back when she was back, and to not bother her again." He blushed. "I've been afraid to call her again, but this is day four, and I admit, I'm a little worried. She rarely takes sick days."

Fiona and I exchanged glances.

"Well, enjoy your little bit of respite," I said, trying not to scare him unnecessarily. "It's probably the flu or something. I know I get cranky when I'm sick. I guess Fiona can give Iris a piece of her mind when she gets back, right, Fiona?"

"Right," Fiona said with an uncertain nod.

"Are you sure I can't interest you in checking out a book today?" Jasper asked. "We just got some new releases, if you enjoy novels."

"Maybe next time," I said. "Thanks, Jasper. We have some errands to run."

"Of course." He bowed again, looking worried.

I took Fiona's arm and led her out of the library, dying to talk to her in private.

"So what are you thinking?" Fiona asked as soon as we got into the truck.

"I'm thinking you're right," I said. "I think Iris really is our treasure hunter. I don't believe for one minute that she's sick, do you?"

"Sick in the head, maybe," Fiona grumbled.

"But I still don't believe she's our murderer," I said. "I know you think she's scrappy, but I just don't see it. And if she's working with the mystery man Jackson is trying to hunt down, she may be in danger. If he's the guy, then he's killed once. Why wouldn't he do it again?"

She nodded, conceding the point.

My phone dinged. I smiled when I pulled it up. Emerson was texting to check on me. I quickly typed out a reply.

I'm with Fiona. We're going to Iris's house, the librarian. She hasn't shown up at the library in 4 days. The earrings were hers. Used to be Fiona's. That's where I had seen them. Long story.

He quickly texted back.

Are you sure you should go alone? Why don't you call Greg to go with you?

I mulled it over for a minute.

I'm pretty sure between the two of us, Fiona and I can take Iris if she tries anything. Seriously doubt Iris is the killer though. She seems pretty frail. I'm just worried she might be in danger.

His response came through almost instantly.

I'm worried YOU are in danger. I know I can't tell you what to do, but I wish you would wait until I could go with you guys. Please be careful. I love you.

I smiled and texted him back.

I love you too. We'll be careful. I promise. I'll text you soon.

Chapter Thirty-Nine

Daphne

Iris lived just a few blocks from the library, so we made quick time to her house. We hopped out of the truck and went to the front door to ring the doorbell.

No answer.

I had a sinking feeling in my gut, but I rang again anyway.

"Oh, I don't like this," Fiona said.

"She may just be out treasure hunting," I suggested, even though everything within me was screaming that wasn't the case.

Fiona gave me a look, letting me know she wasn't buying what I was selling either.

I bit my lip. I had been warned not to break into any more private residences. But Iris might be in trouble, and it wasn't like Fiona would rat me out. I quickly scanned the front porch. There weren't any security cameras in sight.

"Don't tell anyone about this," I warned as I pulled my lock-picking kit from my purse.

Her eyes widened. "Well, Daphne Sullivan, you apparently have a few skills I didn't know about."

"Dad taught me." It hit me for the first time how bad that sounded in light of things. But I shoved that thought out of my mind and focused on the task at hand, grateful when the lock gave easily.

"Ready?" I asked. Fiona nodded. I turned the handle and cautiously opened the door.

The smell hit me before anything else. I didn't have to go any further to know Iris was no longer alive. I stepped back and pulled the door shut.

"I think we're too late," I said.

"Yep," Fiona said with a sigh. "I guess we'd better call the sheriff. Looks like their mystery man struck again."

But something was nagging at me. "Fiona… What if there was no mystery man?"

She frowned. "What do you mean?"

"No one else has seen him. Julie didn't mention him. The only signs they've had of him, at least as far as I know, are some reported sightings and an illegal campsite. But anyone could have faked a campsite and called in some sightings."

"But Jasper said—"

"Exactly."

The realization dawned on her face.

"And," I continued, "he would have known what the journal meant when it said 'the place where men dare not go.' He knew all about the curse."

"We've got to tell Sheriff Morrison."

"Not here," I said. "We need to get out of here. We'll drive straight to the station."

"I'm afraid I can't allow that, ladies." Jasper's cool voice seemed to come out of nowhere. Fiona and I both jumped as he stepped out from the bushes, pointing a pistol straight at us.

"You don't want to hurt us," I said, realizing instantly how stupid it sounded. He had killed two people already. Why would he care about killing us?

"Of course I don't want to hurt you," he said smoothly. "But we have a problem. I knew it the minute you came into the library today looking for Iris. So we'll need to figure out a solution, won't we? I'm glad we have a chance to talk privately. I've been needing to ask you some questions. Shall we go inside?"

Fiona and I exchanged glances.

She eyed him. "Son, I don't know if you realize this, but dead bodies start to *stink* after a day or so. I don't think you want to go in there."

He let out a small sigh. "Well, you'll understand that we need to get out of view of the street. It's one thing for us to be spotted trying to check on Iris. We're concerned friends, after all, aren't we? But it's quite another to be spotted having a long, drawn-out conversation here, especially considering how tempting it might be for either of you to call out for help. So here's what we'll do. We're going to go for a little walk. I'll be a gentleman and take Ms. Fiona's arm, of course. Daphne, you'll answer my questions. Understand?"

With that, he strode right up to Fiona and took her arm, pointing his pistol into her side and raising his eyebrows at me. I knew then that we had to go with him and do what he said. I couldn't risk him hurting her.

"What do you want to know?" I asked flatly.

"I'm glad we understand each other," he said. "Now, walk with me. Keep your hands in sight at all times. I do mean that, Daphne. If I think for even one moment that you're doing anything that would endanger me, I will shoot. You know I will."

"I would never put Fiona in danger."

"I believe you. But even so, keep your hands in sight."

I nodded and began walking beside him, my mind racing as I tried to think of a way out of our predicament. Emerson knew where we had gone. Would he have alerted Greg? Maybe. But would Greg take that seriously or just assume Emerson was being overly protective? I didn't have any way of knowing. All I could do was hope that somehow I would find a way out of this.

"Thank you for your cooperation," Jasper said, adding that slight bow of his. "Question one. Daphne, there are rumors going around that your father stole the treasure. At first I doubted that, but, as you're undoubtedly aware at this point, I've done quite a bit of searching and have come up empty. I know you and your boyfriend were following me on the mountain." He shook his head and clucked his tongue at me, as if I should be ashamed. "So are the rumors true? Did Lonnie Sullivan take my treasure?"

"*Your* treasure?"

"Answer the question."

Fiona yelped as he twisted the pistol into her ribs.

"I'm sorry," I said, holding my hands up. "Please don't hurt her. I was just surprised by your wording. Honestly, I have no idea if my dad found the treasure. I've found no evidence of that, but I also haven't been able to disprove it. I'm not rich, obviously. If he found it, he never told me or my mom anything about it. Emerson and I were on the mountain because we're trying to find the treasure, too. I wouldn't be searching for it if I knew where it was."

He studied my face carefully as I spoke and seemed satisfied by my answer. "I believe you. As you said, why would you be searching for it if you already knew where it was? I doubt he found it. I'm annoyed that I haven't yet, but I think it must still be out there. The whole community has been talking of nothing but Lonnie Sullivan since this whole thing started, which is rather annoying. But that will soon change. The treasure is mine by rights, and everyone will be talking about me soon."

"What do you mean, yours by rights?"

He gave me a patronizing look. "Well, you see, Della Porter was my great-great-great-grandmother. Which means that Kid Curry, of course, was my great-great-great-grandfather.'"

My jaw dropped. "Kid Curry was your ancestor?"

"Apparently so." The pride was evident in his voice. "Of course, I didn't know that until Mr. Adams waltzed into our library doing his research. I had known for some time that Della Porter was my grandmother. Iris and I enjoyed doing genealogical research during our free time at the library. But neither of us had ever dreamed of Della's connection to Kid Curry."

He chuckled. "I don't think Mr. Adams meant to tell me. But when he said he was there researching Della, of course, I was curious. And he did so love to talk about his research. Before he realized it, he had spilled the entire story. Iris and I knew immediately that I was the rightful heir to the treasure, and we made plans to find it."

"So you killed Wesley." It was a statement, not a question.

He shrugged. "It was an interesting experience. Obviously, I couldn't let him find the treasure first. I tried to throw him off the trail by giving him another location for where men dare not go. Bill Brinksley's property," he said with a sideways grin. "Sort of a private joke, since Bill keeps all those no-trespassing signs all over his land. But Iris and I began searching for the true location of the treasure in the *real* place where men dare not go. When Wesley showed up in the clearing, searching there himself, we realized he must have gotten the story about the curse from someone else. So, it had to be done. The treasure is mine. He couldn't find it first."

He lapsed into silence, absentmindedly flexing his free hand. When he spoke again, his tone was oddly introspective. "Before that day, I would never have thought I could kill another human being. But knowing I carried Kid Curry's blood within me made me realize I could be so much more than I ever imagined. It unlocked something inside me —my birthright."

I bit my tongue and swallowed back disgust, staying quiet only because I knew Fiona would pay for it if I voiced my thoughts.

Fiona added a question of her own. "But why did you kill Iris?"

Jasper grinned this time. "Oh, come now, Fiona. Surely you can't tell me you haven't thought of doing the same? Once I realized I had the power within me to kill, I decided I didn't want to share my treasure with her after all. She had made my life miserable for so long. It was well deserved, as I'm sure you would agree."

Fiona huffed.

"Besides," Jasper continued, obviously enjoying the attention. "If I'm being perfectly honest, I was beginning to worry she had found the treasure without me. I made it crystal clear that she was only to search when I was with her, but I found evidence that she was not abiding by that rule. She would have cut me right out had she found it on her own. And that, obviously, couldn't happen."

"What do you think is going to happen now?" I asked before I could stop myself. "You've killed twice. You've kidnapped us. This isn't going to end well for you, Jasper."

He turned to me, a grin lighting up his face. "Don't you see? I'm the new Kid Curry. He, too, killed without regard. He took what he wanted and served no one. I plan to do the same. I'll find the treasure, and when I do, I'll simply disappear. Maybe I'll follow in Butch Cassidy's footsteps and head to South America."

It was clear he had no moral compass left and no fear of getting caught. And by the looks of it, he was walking us away from the center of town straight toward the riverbank, which didn't bode well for our futures. I could only think of one plan. It was a long shot, but if I could make it convincing, and if Fiona played along, maybe I could make it work.

It *had* to work.

Because if it didn't, Fiona and I were about to become the next two victims of Kid Curry's great-great-great-grandson.

CHAPTER FORTY

Daphne

I STOPPED SUDDENLY IN THE ROAD AND CLOSED MY EYES, letting my body sway as if I was disoriented. I put my fingers on my temples and moaned lightly, letting my head rock back and forth.

"What on earth are you doing?" Jasper snapped. I knew without looking that he had the gun pointed at me now.

"Iris," I said in a breathy whisper. "Iris."

"Stop it," he commanded. "You're making a scene."

"The treasure," I moaned, still rocking. "More than she had ever seen. More than she imagined."

"Daphne, I'm warning you," he said, before Fiona interrupted him.

"Can't you see she's having a vision?" she asked. I opened my eyes just in time to see her thump him on the cheek. "Leave her alone. Maybe she'll see where the treasure is."

"A vision?" His tone was uncertain. "What are you talking about?"

I let my hands drop to my side and opened my eyes as wide as I could, hoping I appeared pale and shaken.

"It's true," I said. "I'm psychic. I keep it quiet, but Fiona knows. Joe

Hemsworth does too. How do you think we knew Iris was involved at all? Once she died, I started having visions of her."

He was still uncertain, but I could tell that at least part of him believed me. I had suspected he would. He may have told us about the curse in order to throw us off initially, and he obviously wasn't scared enough of it to stay away from the trail. But the manner in which he had told us that story made me think he was at least a little superstitious. I was hoping that meant he would buy into my "vision."

"What are you saying? You just happened to have a vision of Iris finding the treasure?" His tone was suspicious, but he definitely wanted to believe me.

"Yes. It was...strange." I put my hand back on my head and did my best to look lightheaded. "She was digging on the mountain alone. She found a box and opened it. There were banknotes. More than she could have imagined. She—" I stopped myself, closed my eyes, and started swaying and moaning again. I didn't want to overdo it, but I wanted to really sell the experience.

"It's happening again," Fiona said, backing me up. "Give her some space and for goodness' sake, don't interrupt her again!"

Jasper obeyed, staying quiet this time until I was done. I gave a little gasp and opened my eyes quickly, letting my mouth fall open into a surprised look.

He stared at me. "You know where it is?" It was half question, half statement. He had bought the act.

"Yes," I said. "And I'll tell you. But you have to let us go."

A disappointed look crossed his face. "You don't think I'm that stupid, do you? I thought you really had something there for a minute."

"I don't think you're stupid," I said. "I understand you'll want to get the treasure in hand before you release us. That's only smart. But you have to promise not to hurt us, and that as soon as I lead you to the treasure, you'll let us go."

His eyes flickered with interest as he contemplated my words. "As you wish," he said, making his little bow. "*If* your vision is real, and *if* you can really deliver the treasure into my hands, then I will let you both go unharmed."

I didn't believe him for an instant, but at least I had bought us more time.

"So, where to?" he asked.

"The library."

"The *library?*" Surprise shown on his face.

I nodded. "Of course. Where else would she hide it? She knew you would search her house if you ever got suspicious. And she knew every square inch of that library. She knew the perfect spot."

"*Where* in the library?"

I shook my head. "Not until we get there. You're not stupid, but I'm not either. Trust me, she hid it in the perfect spot. You'll never find it without me, and I'm not telling you where it is while we're out here in the middle of nowhere, where you could just kill us and go get it your-self. If you want it, you'll have to take us to the library. I deliver it into your hands, and you let us walk away. That's the deal."

He raised his eyebrows, then motioned for me to get back in line.

WE WALKED IN SILENCE. All the while, I was trying to figure out how to let someone know where we were. I had left my purse—and phone—in Fiona's truck. Not that Jasper would have actually let me send a text. But without it, I had no idea how to get a message to someone.

I started thinking about how Emerson tracked Jasper through the woods that day. Leaving a trail on a sidewalk was much harder than in the woods, and Emerson was on duty at work. I had no idea if he would come here and see any signs I managed to leave. It was an even bigger Hail Mary than faking the vision. But it was the only thing I could think of. So when we passed by Iris's house again, I started doing what I could to leave signs on the walk to the library.

I started by plucking one of the large flowers growing beside Iris's mailbox. Jasper immediately asked what I was doing, but I played it off.

"I'm nervous," I said. "I just need something to do with my hands, and you said to keep them in sight." I lifted the flower and twirled it in my fingers, acting as if it were a simple fidget device. He frowned but allowed it, so I kept twirling it. Every few steps, I would rip a petal off and let it drop to the ground, praying the wind would stay dead and not blow them away before someone followed us.

Sharp-eyed Fiona immediately picked up on what I was doing. When Jasper's attention was focused on a jogger on the other side of the street, she gave me a look and a head nod to indicate that I should check her sweater pocket. I quickly dipped my hand inside and found a little bag of dried lavender. I slipped it into my own jacket pocket and unrolled the top, so that whenever Jasper was distracted, I could pull out a couple of lavender heads and let them drop to the sidewalk before he noticed.

I did other things too. There were still remnants of snow melting on the side of the sidewalk, dirty from having been pushed there by the plow. Whenever possible, I would step into the wettest, dirtiest parts of it, leaving footprints behind. I took full advantage of a muddy puddle, grateful that the muddy footprints would last longer than the wet ones.

When we passed by a low-hanging branch, I snapped a twig while Jasper wasn't looking, hoping Emerson would see the sign. And when we walked by a metal fence, I allowed it to snag my coat, hoping a piece of fabric would get left behind.

I had no idea if any of these signs would even still be there by the time anyone came looking for us. But it was all I could think of, and I had to give us every chance I could.

THE WALK WAS SHORT, and we soon found ourselves back at the library. Jasper tucked the pistol into the pocket of his blazer, but warned us he wouldn't hesitate to pull it back out and shoot if either of us tried anything. He was, after all, the descendant of Kid Curry, as he enjoyed reminding us.

I didn't doubt him.

"Where to, Ms. Daphne?" he asked with a cruel smile as we stepped inside the library.

I quickly glanced around, trying to come up with the best plan. "I'm not exactly sure," I said. "I know what I'm looking for, but I don't know where it is here. This library is too unfamiliar to me. When I see it, I'll know it. I promise, I won't try anything. But my visions are just small glimpses without a lot of context. I've just got to look until I see the spot I saw in my vision."

His eyes narrowed, but he clamped his lips together and gave a small nod.

I sighed in relief and started walking toward the books, trying to come up with a spot that might give us some sort of advantage over him.

"Just remember," he murmured, following behind me. "I still have Fiona by the arm, so I hope you're telling the truth when you say you won't try anything."

"Scout's honor," I said.

My eyes scanned the room. I walked past the tables and chairs where we had sat before, moving toward the rows of bookshelves. I passed by the first several rows, feeling disheartened. But then I came to a row that gave me an idea.

I paused and put my fingers back up to my head. "Here," I said, turning back to him. "It's here."

He frowned and looked down the aisle. "Here?"

"Yes." I hoped with all my heart that I wasn't about to make a miscalculation and get us killed. "The top row," I said, pointing to a shelf with very old, very *large* reference books of some sort. "She hollowed one of them out and placed the box inside it."

Astonishment shown on his face. "Brilliant," he whispered. "Those never get checked out by patrons, and this section fell under her respon-sibilities, so I never tend to the books here. Absolutely brilliant."

I sighed in relief, grateful he had bought it. I eyed Fiona, who gave me a determined little smile.

"Which book?" he demanded.

I shrugged. "That, I don't know. Like I said, it's a little glimpse. No context. I couldn't tell you where she was on the aisle. We'll just have to look through them."

He grinned and pulled out his gun, making sure we saw it before tucking it back into his pocket. "Well, luckily for me, I can do that myself, ladies. So I'm afraid we're near the end of our journey together.

We'll take another walk, then I'll come back and handle this part alone. I do so appreciate your help, though."

"I wouldn't do that if I were you," Fiona spoke up.

He rolled his eyes. "And why not?"

"Because what if Iris moved it? What if Daphne saw her initial location, but she got paranoid and moved it somewhere else? You know how she was," Fiona pointed out. "I could just imagine her hiding it in ten different places before she felt she had the right one. Can't you? And if she did move it, you might need Daphne's help to find the next spot. She's real connected to Iris right now, having visions left and right. But seems to me they're playing in order, don't you see? Started with her getting involved at all, then her digging, finding it, then putting it here... But what if that's not the end of the trail, so to speak?"

I wanted to hug Fiona for being so quick on her feet.

He frowned but seemed to weigh the possibility. "Fine then," he finally announced. "But I'm afraid that means that you, Daphne, will be the one doing the searching then. I'm not stupid enough to climb up on that ladder and leave you two down here unattended. I will wait below with Ms. Fiona while you search the books."

I nodded and headed up the ladder, catching Fiona's eye as I did. Unspoken communication passed between us, and she gave me an almost imperceptible nod.

I made a big show of opening books and putting them back, going as slowly as I could on the chance that Emerson had called Greg. I would rather have Greg show up than take the chance I was planning on taking. But just in case he didn't, I kept my eye on Jasper, waiting for my chance.

When the first row of books was empty, I moved the ladder down a bit, then headed back up. I repeated this process twice more before noticing that Jasper was getting impatient. I caught Fiona's eye again and knew we were on the same page.

I took another book from the shelf and opened it in a way where Jasper couldn't see what I was seeing. I gave a small gasp and looked down at him.

Just as I hoped, he got excited—so excited that his grip loosened on Fiona. She jerked away from him. I threw the book as hard as I could at his head, followed immediately by as many books as I could knock from the shelf. He lunged toward the ladder, but Fiona was quicker. She pulled the pistol from his pocket, cocked it, and pointed it straight at him.

"Hold up there, Cowboy," she said, sarcasm dripping from her voice. "Looks like you ain't got much Kid Curry in you after all."

CHAPTER FORTY-ONE

Daphne

MOMENTS LATER, FIONA AND I HEARD FOOTSTEPS RUNNING through the building. I was trying to figure out how to explain why I was sitting on a man's back on the library floor while Fiona held a gun on him when Jackson and Emerson rushed around the corner.

"Daphne!" Emerson exclaimed, running to me. He pulled me off of Jasper and into his arms, holding me like he never wanted to let me go again.

"You found us." My heart felt like it might explode with love for him.

"Of course, I found you," he said, setting me back down and holding my face in his hands. "As soon as you texted me where you were going, I had a bad feeling. I called Jackson and told him to head there. I left the base immediately. Jackson was there when I arrived, and so was Fiona's truck, but you two were gone. I saw the trail you left." His face broke out in a grin. "We ran all the way here."

I said nothing, just kissed him as if we were alone in his cabin instead of in the library surrounded by people.

By the time I broke away, Jackson had cuffed Jasper and was calling for backup. Jasper was running his mouth about how it didn't matter. After all, Kid Curry had broken out of jail. So would he! And he would steal Sheriff Morrison's vehicle and drive out of town in it.

Somehow, I seriously doubted that.

Fiona walked over to us, and Emerson wrapped an arm around her, too. "I'm so glad you're both okay," he said, still holding me tightly against him.

"Your girl here is a quick thinker," Fiona said, chuckling. "If not for her, we'd be in the river by now."

I smiled. "That's not entirely true. We make a good team, Fiona. I couldn't have done it without you backing me up."

"Well, of course not, dear," she said. "I'm a mighty fine actress, if I do say so myself."

I grinned and planted a kiss on her cheek.

When Jackson was finally finished questioning us, the three of us headed back to Fiona's house to decompress and fill Emerson in on everything.

"Faking a vision?" he asked, laughing. "Wow. Bold move. But doesn't it worry you that the rumor will spread?"

I shrugged. "A little. But I couldn't think of anything else in the moment. And after all, it really was fake. It's not as if it led to anything except our escape. I'll just play it off as knowing he was superstitious and going with the only thing I could come up with at the time."

He nodded and pulled me closer to him. I couldn't imagine feeling any happier than I did right then. I was safe in Fiona's living room, I was cuddled up with Emerson, Fiona was healthy and not at all worse for wear, and the killer had been caught. All was right with the world.

Well, almost.

After all, there was still a missing treasure out there, and at least one person who believed I owed it to him.

"I'm glad the worst is over," I said, tracing circles on Emerson's chest. "But I wish we had found the treasure. Who knows, though? It may not be out there at all. I just hope that if it's not, it's because Kid and Della really did fake their deaths and run away together. I hope the rumors are true and that they used the money for a fresh start. No more robbery, murder, or prostitution. Just the two of them living their lives together, making babies and growing old somewhere."

Emerson caressed my arm. "Is that what you want?" he asked softly.

My heart sped up, as I wasn't sure if he was talking about Kid and Della, or about us. I hoped, with all my heart, he meant us. But I didn't know if that's what he wanted, and I didn't want to spoil things by putting any unwanted pressure on him. So I decided to play it cool and act as if he was just talking about history.

"Well, obviously, finding the treasure would take some personal stress off of me. But if we can't find it, then yeah, I hope they had a fresh start and a good life. Everyone deserves second chances."

"Well, almost everyone, anyway," Fiona called out from the kitchen.

I giggled.

Emerson reached down and lifted my chin so that I was looking into his eyes.

"I'd say I already found the best treasure right here," he whispered, before leaning down to kiss me.

"Maybe you're right," I agreed.

Epilogue

Daphne

A week later, the treasure was found. Jasper's arrest had drawn even more attention to the hunt, and the mountain had been swarmed with people searching ever since. It was found in a cave, buried below a spot where "KC and DM" were carved into the rock. There wasn't nearly as much of it as everyone had hoped. It was still a nice find, adding up to a current value of nearly two hundred seventy-five thousand dollars. But it wasn't the millions everyone had hoped for, and in the end, it was donated to a local museum...minus a nice finder's fee for the teenager who had discovered it.

I was grateful Dad's name had been cleared and that Bill Brinksley wouldn't be on my back any longer. And, while it may have been a little spiteful, I was also grateful it wasn't found on Bill's land. After all the trouble he had caused me, I was glad he wouldn't reap any rewards.

Jasper admitted to being the one to break into my house. He'd hoped to confirm to himself that I didn't already have the treasure. I was glad to know it was him, both because I was grateful he was being punished for the event that hurt Fiona, and also because I was glad to know it wasn't another Rosemary Mountain resident. I didn't want to look at my neighbors with suspicion.

For a little while, life on Rosemary Mountain returned to normal. As normal as life here can be, anyway. I returned to my cottage, but sometimes stayed at Emerson's when he wasn't working. Sometimes he and Thor would come stay at my place, which was also nice. We were in unknown territory for us, living life as a regular couple without a murder investigation hanging over our heads. I was the happiest I had ever been, and I tried my best to take Fiona's advice to simply love Emerson and not worry about the future or any possible end to our relationship.

I rebuilt my business—not to where it had been, but to a sustainable level that took the pressure off. I was also able to pick up some time working as a temp at the library while they searched for a new librarian. Despite everything, I still loved it there and thoroughly enjoyed the change of pace. And before long, I had a solid offer on Dad's house, giving me a light at the end of the tunnel on my financial stress.

But the peace didn't last long. One cold winter evening, Emerson and I were snuggled up in front of my fireplace, drinking cocoa, when I heard a knock on the door.

"Expecting anyone?" Emerson asked.

"No, not tonight." I put down my mug and went to the door. A wave of anxiety hit me before I even opened it. Somehow, I knew everything was about to change.

I opened the door to find Mom on the doorstep, looking pale.

"Mom? What are you doing here?" I pulled her inside. "Are you sick? What's wrong?" I was so confused. It wasn't like her to travel here without telling me first, and I'd never seen her looking so pale and worried.

"I'm sorry I didn't call you," she began. "But I didn't know what to say. I felt like I just needed to come straight here. That you needed to see this in person."

"What is it, Mom?"

"It's this."

She pulled a journal from her purse and placed it in my hands.

I knew immediately.

This one really was Eileen's.

THANK you for reading the second part of Daphne's story! I hope you enjoyed the adventure. Find out what happens next in *Danger in the Darkness,* where Daphne finally has the clues to take down her mother's killer.

Can't get enough of Rosemary Mountain? Sign up for my mailing list and receive Fiona's Hawthorn Tea recipe. You'll also be the first to know about upcoming releases, sneak peeks, and more!

Reviews are invaluable to authors—they, more than anything, sell books. If you enjoyed Daphne's story, I would so appreciate you taking the time to leave a review at your preferred vendor. It truly means the world.

I would also love for you to come hang out with me on Instagram or Facebook! I love getting to know my readers!

Acknowledgments

As always, my first acknowledgement goes to my husband, Brandon. Writing a book is a strangely emotional, psychological, obsessive experience. Thank you for putting up with me through yet another one. You'll never know how grateful I am to have you by my side. Also, thanks for being my Alpha Reader and for always being honest with me about what works and what doesn't work. I especially appreciate you pointing out that chili was a terrible thing for Emerson to cook on a date that might turn into a sleepover. As a woman, I certainly never would have considered that! As you'll see, I changed it to spaghetti.

Thanks also to my children, for your excitement, your enthusiasm, and your fervent prayers that this book will earn enough money for a trip to Disney World.

Huge thanks to my parents, for your encouragement, for helping plan such a successful launch of the first book in this series, and for your excitement about reading this one–I apologize for giving you yet another cliff-hanger... although, truth be told, I'm not actually sorry at all. Turns out, we writers are kind of mean like that.

I would also like to thank the members of *Cops and Writers* for helping me work out a difficult plot point in this book. I appreciate every law enforcement officer who volunteers their time to answer all of our questions there!

This book made use of some true historical details about Kid Curry and Annie Rogers. I would like to acknowledge Larry Bentley, from the

Appalachian Murder, Mystery, & Legend podcast. I greatly enjoyed your podcast about Kid Curry in Knoxville, and found it so useful in fleshing out this story. I would also like to acknowledge Gary A. Wilson and his book *The Life and Death of Kid Curry,* which was a wealth of information on Curry's life.

I owe a special thanks to Camille Ross, for partnering with me again on the editing process. Your feedback is invaluable and I am so grateful for it!

This beautiful cover, like the one from *Secrets,* was designed by Brooke Passmore of BY THE BROOKE DESIGNS. Brooke, you are incredible to work with, and I'm so lucky to have you on my team!

I would also like to give a very special thanks to Sarra Cannon. Sarra, you'll never know what an encouragement you've been to me on this journey. Your mentorship has made all the difference, and I am truly grateful for you.

Finally, thank you to YOU, to my readers. I was blown away by the response to *Secrets.* You all made the launch of that book absolutely incredible, and I will never forget it. Thank you for forgiving me for the cliffhanger in *Secrets* (and hopefully, for this one as well). Sequels are particularly tough to write when they follow a beloved book, but I hope this book that I've done you proud. Thank you, so much, for your support and love.

About the Author

Nicole Gardner lives in NE Arkansas with her husband, their two sons, and their two crazy dogs. If she's not at her desk, you'll likely find her either in the garden, or creating teas and tinctures in the kitchen.

Nicole's background is in psychology. This fascination with human behavior and relationship dynamics plays a significant role in her writing and the way she shapes her characters.

www.nicolegardnerbooks.com